SUMMERTIME NIGHTS

A KATAMA BAY SERIES

KATIE WINTERS

Summertime Nights
A Katama Bay Series
By
Katie Winters

CHAPTER ONE

THIRTY YEARS EARLIER

ELEVEN-YEAR-OLD CARMELLA PRESSED a finger against her lips to silence Colton, her younger brother, who was ten. They stood off to the side of Elsa's bedroom as their older sister slept on. Her hair was spread out, so angelic, across the pillows, and her sheets were a mess. Probably, she'd had one of her frequent nightmares, ones that had previously made Elsa crawl into their mother and father's bed. For the past years, Carmella knew Elsa had fought her nightmares alone — telling herself that she wasn't allowed to sleep in her parents' bed. She was the eldest; she had to be stronger than that.

It was just a few days into their summer vacation. Carmella and Colton — absolute best friends and frequent mischievous companions had decided to decorate Elsa's bedroom. They wanted to cheer her up since Elsa's boyfriend had dumped her for no apparent reason. He'd said he wanted to be single for summer vacation. To Carmella, a breakup seemed very adult, and it broke

1

her heart to see her sister so despondent. She wanted to grab her and tell her they were still kids— that they didn't have to endure all the heartache of adults yet.

The decorating process had gone on the past thirty minutes. Colton and Carmella had hung streamers, balloons and self-made posters across Elsa's bedroom. On the posters, they'd drawn cartoons and words like "HAPPY SUMMER VACATION!" and "SCHOOL'S OUT!" To Carmella and Colton, these posters were absolute works of art. They beamed with pride at the décor; they couldn't imagine a world in which Elsa wouldn't look at it all and think, "Okay. I'll be fine."

That moment, Elsa stirred beneath the sheets. Her beautiful eyes popped open. Colton giggled, and Elsa swung her head around to look at him.

"What are you doing in my room?" she demanded. She rose up from the pillows, blinked into the dim light of the morning, then gasped. "What the heck did you guys do?"

Carmella's heart sank. She knew this wasn't Elsa's "pleased" voice. In fact, she sounded enraged, like the time Carmella had eaten almost all of her Halloween candy, the pieces she'd been saving.

Elsa leaped from bed, placed her hands on her hips, and looked at the posters, the streamers, the balloons.

"Are you kidding me?" she demanded. "This will take forever to clean up."

Colton dropped his chin to his chest. He was a terribly sensitive kid and frequently cried, which was something that frustrated their father, Neal, as he'd always wanted a son, but not one who was weak. He was only ten — there was still time for him to become a strong man. But as usual, parents were impatient.

"We just wanted to decorate for summer," Colton said softly.

Elsa yanked her head around and glared at them. She heaved a sigh, then said, "Just get out of my room, okay?"

Colton and Carmella remained there, their hands at their sides. This had gone off the rails. Carmella gaped at her big sister, a girl she loved with every vibrant beat of her heart.

"GET OUT!" Elsa cried then.

Carmella and Colton leaped into action. They burst from Elsa's bedroom and scampered down the hall. Their mother, Tina, stood at the end of the hallway with a stack of towels in hand. She balked at them and said, "What on earth have you gotten yourselves into?"

Colton tore into his bedroom and fell on his bed. A sob escaped his throat as he shook against the mattress. Carmella paused in the doorway as her mother stepped alongside her.

"Colton! Tell me what's wrong?" Tina asked tenderly.

Elsa stormed into the hallway after that. "Don't let them butter you up, Mom."

"Elsa. Whatever it was, it's obvious your brother is very upset about it," Tina said.

"They broke into my room, Mom. They destroyed everything."

Tina arched an eyebrow toward Carmella. "Is that true, Carm?"

Carmella shrugged. "We just wanted to cheer her up."

Their father, Neal, appeared in the doorway of their parents' bedroom. He rubbed his eye sleepily. In recent days, he'd had a cold, and his grogginess permeated through his voice. "What's going on out here?"

"The kids have wasted no time in getting in an argument," Tina

3

explained. She stepped toward Neal and dotted a kiss on his cheek as he protested.

"Don't! I don't want to get you sick."

"I think you're better already," Tina said. "Come on, everyone. Whatever happened, there's nothing that can't be fixed with pancakes. Grab your dirty laundry from your bedrooms and leave it in the laundry room. And Elsa?"

Elsa furrowed her brow and glared at her mother.

"Your brother and sister love you. And we love you, too. Try to be a little nicer next time."

Elsa rolled her eyes into the back of her head. Again, Carmella was struck with the knowledge that soon, Elsa would be a full-flung teenager. Carmella was right up behind her in age. Childhood was somehow fleeting; she'd never imagined it would end before.

Tina poured maple syrup over their pancakes and set out a jug of juice on the table on the back porch. Colton hadn't yet grown into himself, and his legs didn't reach the floor. His feet wagged around beneath him as he dove into the pancakes. Elsa placed several napkins alongside his plate and said, "You're going to need these."

When Colton blinked up, his chin was already slathered in syrup. Neal grumbled to himself. Probably, their parents were more ready for them not to be kids than Carmella could really understand.

When they'd finished, Tina suggested that they take the horses out. It was a beautiful morning, and Neal didn't have anything going on at the Katama Lodge and Wellness Spa until later that afternoon.

"I think it would be nice if we all did something as a family," Tina suggested. "Something to celebrate summer vacation!"

In recent years, Neal and Tina had built up a hefty collection of horses. Carmella always loved stepping into the stables; she loved the shadows of the horses' noses as they poked them out into the hay-lined hall; she even loved the smell of their shiny coats and the grunts they made, which seemed to be their personal greetings.

Carmella scampered up to the glossy white beauty she so frequently rode, the one she'd named "Ghost." Colton took the brown horse alongside Ghost, which they'd named Marvin a few years back. Elsa opted for Black Beauty while their parents took out two horses from the far end of the stables. It took quite a bit of time to prepare for the ride. Neal seemed overly frustrated with the process. As he slid a saddle over the back of one of the horses, he grumbled to himself and then started to cough.

"Maybe you aren't well enough to ride?" Tina suggested.

Neal cast her a strange look, then said, "Tina, you're the one who wanted us all to ride together."

Carmella turned her eyes to the ground. Parents fought; she knew this. She just hated when hers did.

"Don't talk to me like that," Tina whispered.

Immediately, Neal apologized. In a few minutes, he'd adjusted the last saddle. And in another few minutes more, all of the horses were ready to go.

Carmella lifted her chin and held the reins loosely, the way she'd learned from her father. They clopped forward in a line — Neal at the front, Elsa behind him, Tina in front of Colton, and Carmella in the very back. They had just shy of one hundred acres of land, which stretched along the southern edge of the island and met up with the Katama Lodge and Wellness Spa, which was located eastward, along Katama Bay. For Carmella, Elsa, and Colton, their acreage was essentially the entire world; they wanted for nothing more but these salty waves, the rush of the wind, and the creak of the trees in their dense forest.

Colton hadn't fully recovered yet from Elsa's anger that morning. He rode with his back curved and his chin downward and frequently, Carmella heard his throat wheeze with sadness.

They rode for nearly an hour. Carmella was very quiet, lost in her thoughts. She thought about Elsa, about whether or not Elsa would stop loving her and Colton as she grew older. She thought about her best friend Cody and his older sister; she'd taken to screaming at him for everything, even for talking to her. Would Elsa do that to her? Would Elsa make her feel like she only annoyed her all the time?

Was it possible that in this life, you couldn't even trust the people you loved to love you back? The thought filled Carmella with dread.

They paused near the shoreline, where the forest filtered out toward the sands. Neal gazed out across the waters. Carmella wondered what was on her father's mind. Throughout her childhood, he had been one of her favorite people — and yet, she'd always found him to be a mystery.

Carmella's horse clambered forward the slightest bit. She glanced left toward Colton's horse. There, on the back end of the horse, sat an enormous horsefly. Its green coloring glittered in the sunlight.

On instinct, Carmella reached over and smashed her hand against the hind of Colton's horse. Before she could get it, the horsefly buzzed off. But her impact frightened the horse. Immediately, the horse bucked forward, leaping wildly toward the water's edge, whinnying and out of control. Its eyes were full of fear.

Colton panicked as he clutched the reins for dear life and cried out. "MOM!"

"Colton! Oh my God!" Tina leaped from her horse and rushed for Colton's horse.

But Colton's horse had worked itself into a tizzy. Carmella's heart burst into her throat. She had never seen a horse so wild. After another moment, the horse bucked back again, whipped its front legs into the air, and cast Colton back onto the rocks. The horse then smashed his legs onto Colton's chest.

The sound was so menacing. Carmella had never heard anything like it.

Tina's wails swept across the waves. Neal had jumped off his horse already and grabbed the reins of Colton's wild horse as Tina fell to her son's side and continued to cry out. Elsa and Carmella jumped off their horses; neither remembered to hold onto their reins and their horses cantered off.

Colton's face was terribly pale. Carmella had never seen him like that. The back of his head had smacked against one of the stones along the beach, and the impact of the horse's hooves had torn his shirt. His chest was bruising quickly. Blood had begun to spill out from his mouth. He sputtered and gazed up into his mother's eyes. He looked so frightened, so lost, as though he'd was confused from a dream.

"Colton! Colton. Can you hear me? Oh, baby. Please..." Tina cried.

Carmella lost all the feeling in her arms and legs. A moment later, she fell to the ground and watched as her baby brother, one of her best friends on the planet, escaped the soft grip of the world and fell into death.

Even though Neal knew he was gone, he rushed into the house to call the ambulance. Elsa stood on the rocks in shock while tears streamed down her face. Tina brought Colton's frail body against her chest and shook back and forth. Carmella remained on the ground; she was rooted to her spot and felt unable to do anything at all.

This was the space in the world where her brother had last been alive.

And it was her fault.

She'd sent the horse into a wild panic.

And the horse had cast Colton to his death.

And maybe Carmella already intuitively knew that her life had changed forever. Maybe she could sense it in the way the air shifted, in the way the water crept onto the sands, in the way her mother's sharp eye turned toward her with the first sign of resentment.

Their family would never be the same again.

CHAPTER TWO

TWO YEARS LATER

THIRTEEN.

Carmella was thirteen years old and generally anxious about it. She was worried about the wild and provocative years that seemed to stretch forth, the years of having to shave her legs, getting her period and dare she say it— flirting with boys. She stood in the middle school bathroom and shifted herself the slightest bit to catch sight of the beginning curves of her body, curves that made her both nervous and proud. Elsa, her sixteen-year-old sister, seemed entirely confident and at ease in her body. Carmella hoped that someday soon, she would feel the same.

A head poked around the corner of the bathroom. "Carm? You're taking forever."

"Get out!" Carmella teased as she rushed toward the door. Her best friend, Cody, waited for her in the hallway. They'd planned to head to the diner after school for milkshakes and jukebox plays and a mountain of French fries. This was something of a ritual, as neither of them was particularly keen on heading home after school.

It was October and as they walked to the diner, the air bit at their cheeks and reminded them of the coming winter. Tree leaves were tinged orange and red and yellow. Cody discussed his recent foray into the math academic team, which he was generally embarrassed about. "I don't want everyone to think I'm super nerdy, you know?"

Carmella giggled. "But Cody, you are super nerdy. The sooner we all accept this, the better off we'll be."

"Gee. Thanks." He gave her that look again — one that sent a funny shiver down Carmella's spine. Carmella lifted her chin and shoved the thought far back into her mind. Cody was her only friend; she wouldn't do anything to mess that up.

At the diner, Cody put on a song by TLC and did a little dance at the front of the table. One of the diner waitresses smoked a cigarette in the corner. She looked at them as though they'd ruined her afternoon. It was three-twenty and the dinner rush wasn't for hours. Due to the fact that they were thirteen, they had very little money for a tip.

When their milkshakes arrived, Cody sucked his straw too hard and got an immediate brain freeze. Carmella chortled with laughter, then paid herself back with a brain freeze of her own.

"See what happens when you make fun of people?" Cody teased.

"Ah, it's not fair!" Carmella cried.

"The world is an unfair place," Cody affirmed.

Carmella knew this all too well. It wasn't something she discussed often — the fact that her brother had died two years before, but it was something Cody knew inside and out. In the wake of the incident, Carmella had put so much blame on herself that the trauma had almost ripped her in half. She had struggled to eat properly since then. Her mother, father, and older sister hardly looked her way. It was her fault, after all, that Colton had died. She had been the one to smack the horse's back end. It was all on her and she felt the enormity of it weigh down on her shoulders.

Silence fell at the table. Cody placed his hands to the right of his milkshake. He seemed unwilling to look up.

"Have you talked to your parents about what I said last week yet?" he finally asked.

Carmella heaved a sigh. "I just don't even want to talk to them about anything. Let alone therapy."

Cody shrugged. "I think it would be really good for you. You went through something really traumatic, something really awful."

Carmella's cheeks burned. She placed her lips around her straw and sucked again. The jukebox changed to a David Bowie song, and she bobbed her shoulders around. In the corner, the diner waitress grumbled, apparently not a fan.

"Just talk to them. Please," Cody said. "Maybe they would understand more than you're giving them credit for."

———

LATER THAT NIGHT, Carmella watched her mother in the large rocking chair by the window. The October sky had grown violent and purple, and large raindrops plastered themselves across the glass. Her mother had a large quilt spread over her lap. The needle flickered with the light from the lamp overhead. Nobody had said a word for over forty-five minutes. Carmella was meant to be focused on her homework, but in reality, her heart ached with sorrow. Her mother said the words, "I love you," but it had been a long time since Carmella had fully felt she meant them.

Elsa padded in from the kitchen. She held a gummy worm in hand and she wagged her eyebrows at Carmella. "Do you want to paint your nails?" she asked.

Carmella nodded, placed her books to the side and rushed upstairs with Elsa. It was a rare thing that her older sister allowed Carmella any time in her bedroom. As Carmella passed by Colton's room, a shiver rushed over her. That happened every single time. She hadn't opened Colton's door in many months, but the last time, she had found the room exactly the same as though they'd decided to keep it like a tomb.

When the door was closed in Elsa's room, Carmella sat on the floor against the bed and watched as Elsa went through her immense nail polish collection. The little bottles clanked against one another gently; it was like music. As Elsa placed out a blue, a turquoise, a pink, and a red for Carmella to choose, Carmella found her voice. Her question surprised her.

"Why don't you think Mom and Dad ever talk about Colton?"

Elsa's eyes drew toward Carmella sharply. She dropped her shoulders. "I think it hurts them too much."

"It hurts me, too. But I think it's way worse to pretend that he never existed," Carmella offered.

"I don't think that's what they're doing, Carm. I hear them crying at night," Elsa said.

Carmella's heart dropped into her stomach. She had a flashing image of herself — two years before — crying that it was all her fault, that she'd killed Colton. Her parents had said, "No, no. It's not. It's not your fault. It was just an awful accident." so many times, but she had never fully believed them. She wasn't sure they'd believed themselves, either.

"Cody says that I should go to therapy," Carmella blurted out.

The color instantly drained from Elsa's face. "Why are we talking about this? Don't you want to paint your nails?" She stood and sauntered toward her boom box, where she placed a Madonna CD in the center, then cranked the sound. This was Carmella's cue to shut up.

Tina arrived about twenty minutes later. She peered in through the doorway, placed her head on the door frame, and said, "Look at my beautiful girls, hanging out together."

Carmella hadn't heard her mother compliment her in what felt like years. She beamed up and flashed her hand around.

"You went with turquoise, huh?" Tina asked. "Bold color."

"Carmella wants to be bold in every area of her life," Elsa said. "She took the Seventeen magazine quiz that says she's a strong, confident woman."

"Is that so?" Tina buttoned her cardigan toward her neck and tried on a smile that didn't quite fit her face. "I'm going to run to the store. Do you girls want anything? Candy? Chips? Pop?"

"Twizzlers, please!" Carmella cried.

"Nothing for me," Elsa said. She then cast Carmella a look and added, "When you get to be my age, you'll learn how to watch your figure."

"Don't listen to her, Carm," Tina said. "Eat as many Twizzlers as you want. Life is too short."

Tina made her way downstairs. She hollered out for their father and said, "I'll be home in a bit." Then, there was the sound of the door and the latch as it closed.

Carmella lost herself in Elsa's bedroom after that. She painted her other hand, laid on the floor, and then listened as Elsa spoke on the phone with one of her best friends, who'd just broken up with her boyfriend and was inconsolable. When Elsa got off the phone, she sighed and said, "You won't believe the kind of stuff you'll have to put up with when you're my age, Carm. It's like boys become total foreign entities."

Carmella tried to imagine Cody becoming like that. He was her everything; they knew one another inside and out — at least, it seemed like. What exactly did Elsa mean?

A few minutes after Elsa hung up the phone, the house phone rang. Elsa and Carmella continued to hang out; they figured Neal would grab it downstairs. After three rings, he did. And for a long time, Carmella didn't think anything of it. People called all the time. Ninety-nine percent of the time, they didn't call with bad news.

Everything happened at once after that. It was kind of a blur. Even as Carmella lived through it, she found herself discovering flashbacks of the time after Colton had died. The two eras lived in parallel.

Their father appeared in the doorway. He wore his coat and quickly blurted out that he had to leave the house. That he would call when he knew more. Both Elsa and Carmella looked at each other confused and scared. They sensed something was off immediately.

"Where is Mom?" Elsa asked.

Neal's eyes were like stone. "I'll call you when I know more."

Elsa and Carmella stood downstairs and watched the rain. Their father didn't call; in the end, one of his friends and co-workers from the Lodge, a woman named Tatiana, came to the house. Her eyes were rimmed red with tears.

"Where is Mom? Where's our dad?" Elsa demanded.

"Your dad is at the hospital," Tatiana said somberly. "Your mother was in a very bad car accident."

It was only then that Carmella realized she had built up a wall around her heart. When her mother hadn't arrived home in time, it was like her body had already assumed the worst. Elsa's wails bounced from wall to wall in their large kitchen, but Carmella remained silent and in shock. How could this be happening again?

They stayed awake until their father arrived home around one in the morning. He couldn't fully say the news, but Carmella and Elsa already assumed the worst. They knew their mother was gone. They shared a bed that night, the two sisters, and stared into the darkness above. Carmella knew Elsa wasn't sleeping, just as Elsa probably knew she wasn't, either. Still, there was nothing to be said, only tears to be shed.

Carmella cursed herself in the days leading up to and after the funeral. She cursed that the last memories she really had of her mother were filled with dread and sorrow. They hadn't shared many laughs since Colton's death. Carmella had felt like an alien in her own home. Her mother's death wasn't her fault, but she somehow took on the guilt anyway. Maybe, if she hadn't killed Colton, her mother wouldn't have gone out to the store that night. Maybe, if she hadn't killed Colton, her mother would have felt comfortable enough to sit with Elsa and Carmella and paint her nails and gossip about teenage boys. Just maybe.

Carmella found herself swimming in a sea of maybes.

Neal was inconsolable until he wasn't. By the time Carmella turned fourteen, he was a bit brighter, a bit more confident. He still struggled to look either of his girls in the eye, although Carmella could sense that Elsa and Neal were growing increasingly closer. Carmella was surprised to find that she felt like she just didn't fit in even more than she had prior to her mother's death. Again, Cody begged her to ask for therapy, but the concept felt so strange to her.

"My entire family needs therapy. I guess we'll just go crazy together," she joked.

They'd watched the years pass. Their broken family held none of the luster and warmth of previous years. When Carmella looked at old photographs of the five of them, she felt as though that was some other family living some other life, with very different thoughts and priorities. She couldn't envision them in that reality at all. She supposed it was similar for Neal and Elsa, as well.

It was only when Karen came into their lives that Carmella felt that first sigh of relief. Finally, someone saw her. Finally, someone wanted to include her. It was the "warmth" of the family she'd missed so much. And she clung onto it for dear life — until it, too, was gone for good.

CHAPTER THREE

THE PRESENT

IT WAS EARLY AUGUST — a steamy day of impenetrable sunlight and glittering Katama Bay waters. Carmella stood at the far end of the acupuncture table and adjusted her ponytail. In the hallway in the Katama Lodge and Wellness Spa, she could hear the soft laughter of Janine, her stepsister, as she joked with Mallory, Carmella's niece, who had recently begun to work as the receptionist. It warmed Carmella's heart to feel these new connections brewing which was a sensation that Carmella didn't know well. After all, she had spent most of the previous thirty years closing people off, brewing in her own self-hatred, fighting to take care of herself and only herself.

In recent weeks, all of that had changed, but Carmella knew better than to guess that years and years of trauma and pain would just fade away like that. Sure, she and Elsa had found common ground for the first time since their teenage years; but that didn't mean Carmella fully trusted her. The love she had always had for her sister brewed stronger and bubbled up to her heart. But in her core, Carmella had the sense that she was alone and would always be alone. Probably, that would never go away.

There was a rap at the door. Carmella headed over and opened it to find Elsa herself. She wore a black button-down dress, and her face was vibrant.

"Somebody looks like they had a great date last night," Carmella said, giving her sister a once-over.

Elsa blushed. She stepped inside — into Carmella's space, something she so rarely did and sighed deeply. "I don't know. Is it too soon?"

Carmella shook her head. "I don't think so. But only you know that for sure."

"Right. I know that. And I also love that Bruce gets it, you know? He lost his wife, too. But there's still so much we can't say to one another. I don't want to tell him everything about Aiden, about our life together."

"And you don't have to. Not ever. You can keep some of that sacred," Carmella returned.

Elsa nodded. "It's strange, you know. Dating at forty-five. In some ways, I feel like a dried-up prune, and in others, I feel so free and alive and hopeful for the future."

Carmella laughed. Elsa sounded a lot like the women who breezed in and out of the Lodge, on the hunt for healing, renewal and growth. They weren't sure how to grab the things in life they wanted the most, but they knew there was no other option but to leap.

This "leaping" was something Carmella understood on paper. It was nothing she had ever managed to do herself.

"Anyway, I wanted to stop in before you head off," Elsa said. "I think it's so cool that you've set aside time for this clinic."

Carmella nodded. "I can't believe it, really. It's a little spontaneous for my liking."

"But you love the southwest," Elsa offered. "It'll be so strange to be back, right? After all these years away."

"Sure," Carmella replied. "I did a lot of growing up while I was there. I wonder if I'll still feel my old self there at all."

"We never really grow up, do we? We just get older," Elsa offered. "Which reminds me. I'm headed to Mila's esthetician salon this week. I have to tend to some of these lines." She pointed to the barely seen crow lines at the corner of her eyes.

"You're just as youthful as a daisy," Carmella said.

"Now, I know that isn't true for a minute," Elsa returned. After a beat, she asked, "What time is Cody picking you up?"

"In about twenty minutes, I guess. It's really kind of him to drive me to the airport."

"You know he'd do anything for you," Elsa said. "He always has."

Carmella shrugged gently. "He's just a really good guy."

Cody's SUV pulled up to the Katama Lodge and Wellness Spa three minutes early. Carmella placed her suitcase in the back seat, alongside the car seat that normally held his toddler. As usual, the car smelled of sticky snacks and diapers. Cody had long since given up on apologizing for it. He frequently said, "This is just my life now," and Carmella laughed.

"Hey, hey!" Carmella said as she buckled herself into the passenger seat.

"Hey there." Cody beamed at her. He was forty-two, just like she was, with this dark brown beard and curly dark locks. His green eyes were the same as they'd always been, just lined with the slightest of laugh lines. "How's your day going so far?"

"Not bad. I had two appointments this morning."

"I love that you just poke people with needles all day," Cody proclaimed. "It's like you're a torture enthusiast."

"Excuse me. I promote only healing and wellness," she teased.

"Yeah, yeah. But I know why you really got into it. Sadism," he returned with a smile.

Carmella planned to fly out from the Boston airport. Cody eased his car onto the ferry, parked in the belly of the beast, and then led Carmella up to the little bistro, where he ordered himself a beer and her a glass of wine. They sat in the splendor of the sun. As usual, they said, "This is the last year we can sit in the sun like this. It's going to damage our skin." And as usual, they made no motion to leave their spot.

"How is Gretchen doing?" Carmella asked.

"Oh, you know. Being three is hard work," Cody jested. "She got into a fight with a little boy at the babysitter's and apparently, Fiona had to go pick her up. She wouldn't stop crying."

"Oh no. Did you bring another sensitive little creature into the world?" Carmella asked.

"It really seems like it," Cody replied, leaning into his chair. "I should have known better. Life is hard enough."

When they got back in the car and drove out of Woods Hole, Fiona, Cody's ex-wife, called them on speaker.

"Hey there." Fiona's voice was hard and stern. Carmella couldn't remember if she'd always been like that.

"Hi! What's up?" Cody, as usual, was bright and accommodating.

"I just wanted to let you know that Gretchen has a stomach bug," Fiona said. "She threw up all afternoon. I'm going to need you to take her tomorrow since she can't go to the babysitter's and I have an entire day of meetings."

"That's fine," Cody affirmed.

"Where are you? Am I on speaker?" Fiona asked.

Cody adjusted his hands on the wheel. He looked suddenly nervous. "I think I told you. I'm bringing Carmella to the airport."

There was silence. Carmella's throat constricted.

"Maybe you did. I can't remember," Fiona finally said. "Hi, Carmella. I guess you can hear me?"

"Hi Fiona," Carmella replied. She felt terribly uncomfortable. "How have you been?"

"Oh, fine. The usual chaos of raising a toddler."

"Yeah. I guess it's rough."

"Think long and hard before you have one of your own," Fiona returned. After a beat, she added, "I mean, not that you were thinking about it at all. Women can make all kinds of choices."

Carmella was forty-two years old. She had never been given a chance to think about such things. She felt herself shrink in her seat.

"Thanks for the heads up," she said.

"I'll pick up Gretchen this evening, actually," Cody said. "So you can prep for those meetings."

"Really? That would be so fantastic." Fiona breathed a literal sigh of relief. "I'll see you later, then. Text me when you're back on the island."

After they hung up, Carmella and Cody held the silence for a while. Carmella glanced at her nails and realized she had chipped one of them that morning — something she might have to rectify when she got to the Southwest, as she didn't want to seem clumsy to the other people at the clinic.

"I'm sorry to hear Gretchen doesn't feel well," Carmella finally said.

"That's kids, I guess. It's always one thing after another."

Carmella nodded. "Fiona sounds stressed."

"She's always like that."

"Yeah, I guess."

"I mean, I didn't think she was when we got married," Cody offered. "Maybe I was the one who made her stressed. Who knows?"

Carmella had, of course, heard the ins and outs of Cody's very brief marriage to Fiona. They had met when Cody and Carmella had both been thirty-five. Fiona had been thirty-two and very ready for marriage and babies. Cody had had a few semi-serious relationships over the years, but nothing that became solid. When Fiona had said, "Let's do it," he'd agreed.

In the wake of that decision, he had fallen into an era of heartbreak. After the wedding, they'd had maybe a month or two of marital bliss before the fighting began. They'd already discussed divorce by the time Fiona ended up pregnant. They had decided to stick it out for the baby and then, by the time Gretchen had turned one, Cody had decided to move out. It had been a struggle for them both. Carmella was, of course, on Cody's side, but she also had empathy for Fiona's situation. It wasn't like the universe handed you a how-to manual. *How to have a happy marriage,* or *"how to* be a mother," or "how to handle the intricacies of a divorce while caring for a toddler."

"Never get married, Carmella," Cody said with a grumbling sigh then. "It's nothing but heartache."

Carmella allowed herself to laugh, even though she didn't feel it. She turned her head to the side and watched the side of the road, where the pavement disappeared up against the grass.

"At least that little girl is worth it," Carmella finally added, as she didn't like the silence to stretch out so thin.

"Oh, God. She really is," Cody affirmed. "You should hear some of the new words she came up with the other day."

"She's a smart little thing like you were. Remember when you were doing math academic team?"

"Yes, I do. I was such a nerd. Hopefully, she doesn't follow in those footsteps," Cody chuckled.

"I don't know. Being a nerd suited us both," Carmella admitted as she looked out the window twirling a piece of her hair. "Nobody needed us, and we didn't need them, either."

"It was just us against the world," Cody said with a smile. "That's right."

CHAPTER FOUR

THE FIRST TIME Carmella had embarked to the Southwest to hone a career in acupuncture, she'd been a new high school graduate. Her father hadn't approved of the decision. He'd made that very clear on more than one occasion. But at the time, he'd just wanted her out of his life. She was a significant reminder of so many things: Colton's death, Karen's volatility, and Tina's accident. He had kept Elsa by his side; even as she'd had her babies and built a life with Aiden, she had committed fully to being Neal's business partner. This had left very little space for Carmella on the island.

After Carmella's training in the Southwest, she had returned to the island but not without trepidation. She simply hadn't known where else to turn. In the wake of Karen's absence, the Katama Lodge had lacked an acupuncturist, and Neal and Elsa had offered her the position. There had been resentment in Neal's eyes when he'd agreed to it. Elsa had said it wasn't so, but at the time, Carmella hadn't trusted Elsa to tell the truth.

Now, Carmella stepped off the plane in New Mexico as a very different woman. Forty-two years old and much more self-assured, at least she hoped so. She collected her luggage and hailed a taxi. As she watched the driver place her suitcase in the trunk, she lifted her cheeks toward the sunlight. "It's different here than out east," she told him as she got in. "The heat is so dry, and it's difficult to breathe."

"I've never lived anywhere else," the driver told her. He got in and then lifted his hands to the steering wheel. He wore turquoise jewelry, the likes of which were tremendously popular out there. Carmella remembered that she had worn her own share of it in her youth. She had no idea where those pieces were these days; she'd lost them along the way.

Carmella relaxed for a while in her hotel room. She put some of her dresses and skirts and blouses in the closet and liked the way they looked, hanging like that, as though she'd transplanted her life to a new realm. Cody texted her just past six in the evening to ask how everything had gone.

CARMELLA: Not bad. It's so hot! We have a welcome dinner at seven-thirty. Guess it's time to mingle.

CODY: Mingling. Your favorite thing!

CARMELLA: Maybe I can learn to like it. Who knows? Maybe we can grow and change in adulthood.

CODY: Gosh, I hope so. :)

The acupuncture clinic was held at the very school Carmella had gone to twenty years earlier. Carmella stepped into the main hallway and was surprised to find that much of the space was exactly the same. They'd even stuck with the horrible light green walls. On the far end, there were a number of photographs of the various graduating classes. She found hers in the middle. There she stood, the front row, off to the right. She looked youthful and bright and happy. If only she'd actually felt that way at the time. It was funny what old photographs seemed like, compared to the reality.

Carmella recognized a few people from her class as they ambled into the larger reception hall. She greeted a woman named Clara, who she'd always liked back in the old days. Now, Clara told her, she had an acupuncturist clinic in Seattle and enjoyed a very comfortable life. "I got married around age thirty, but we never had children," she explained. "Just three dogs. They're my world."

Carmella sidestepped any feelings of jealousy. Sure other people had moved on and built their lives. It hadn't been something she had ever been able to do and that was okay. It had to be okay.

Carmella grabbed a glass of wine and sat in the crowd. There were to be a number of announcements about the following few days of the clinic, along with several guest speakers. She was surprised to find herself excited. This was a good next step in her career; she was there for the singular reason that she wanted to push herself forward and become a better version of herself professionally.

The new president of the acupuncturist school stepped to the center of the stage and greeted everyone. "I'm happy to say that I've been the president of this school for the past four years, and within that time, we've taught hundreds of wonderful acupuncturists in this ancient medicinal practice. It's been a unique pleasure. And now, with so many of you grads back, I see the wonderful work this school has done for people all over the world. Anyone who's ever practiced acupuncture knows that it's a wonderful practice of endless gratefulness."

The crowd applauded. The man set his jaw, smiled, then continued on.

"We have a very good schedule crafted for you over the next few days. Conversations and speeches and clinics that will assuredly round out your practices all over the forty-six states you represent. I think we even have a few countries represented, correct? France? Yes? And Belgium?"

There was more applause. Carmella's heart ballooned. She was a part of a bigger mission. She was a piece of a greater puzzle. It was all so beautiful. It felt so right.

"Now, without further ado, I want to introduce you to one of our most important speakers for this year's clinic," he continued. "She came to this clinic years and years ago, has been a frequent guest lecturer, and continues to have her own acupuncture center in Wisconsin. I've asked her over and over again through the years, why Wisconsin? And she just tells me she got tired of the desert."

Everyone chuckled. Carmella joined in.

"Now, everyone, please give a warm welcome to Karen Brosnahan," the president said. "My dear friend and a prominent acupuncturist in her own right."

Carmella stopped breathing for a full twenty seconds. She kept her hands plastered to her thighs as a familiar woman marched out onto the stage. There she stood: Karen, the woman her father had married so many years ago and the mother figure Carmella had latched onto during some of the darkest moments of her life. This woman had altered Carmella's relationship with Elsa in nearly every conceivable way. And when Neal had divorced her, Carmella had struggled to forgive him, as she'd felt it was a direct rebuke of her comfort, her love.

"Good evening, everyone." Karen beamed up into the crowd. "Thank you for the warm welcome. I always love returning to the Southwest. It's where I got my start. It's where I learned about this beautiful field. And when I come back here, I always feel this previous version of myself — a young girl who was largely clueless but brave enough to take hold of her life and make things happen."

Karen was in her sixties but still just as beautiful as she'd been twenty years before. Her hair was grey-blonde, and she remained slender and chic. As usual, her fashion was on point, yet she had aged it up appropriately. Carmella had always been impressed with her stylistic ability; she'd always evoked charm in everything she'd done. Elsa had called this "manipulative," but Carmella hadn't believed it for a second.

And even now, as Karen spoke, Carmella's heart surged with love. Once you loved someone, it never really went away. She'd always believed that.

Carmella couldn't concentrate. She hardly heard what Karen said. Suddenly, she realized she'd joined the rest of the audience in applause — then stood up with the rest of them and headed back to the reception hall. She paused near the back of the hall and glanced back to make sure Karen would follow. She had to speak with her.

When Karen appeared in the doorway, she was still in conversation with the president. If Carmella had to guess, the president had a crush on her. And why shouldn't he? Karen was beautiful.

Carmella waited a few feet away from her ex-stepmother. She couldn't help but compare her current feelings for Karen with her newfound feelings for Nancy. She and Nancy had just never really connected; Nancy had fallen head-over-heels with Elsa, and nothing else had mattered, it had seemed like. Yes, there was room for Carmella and Nancy's relationship to bloom and maybe it would, in time.

Karen tilted her head the slightest bit as her eyes landed on Carmella. Her lips parted in surprise. She lifted a finger to the president and said, "I have to step away for a moment." She then snapped over to Carmella as though Carmella was a magnet.

"My dear. You look positively stunning," Karen said.

Carmella's cheeks burned with excitement. "As do you."

Carmella nodded as her eyes filled with tears. She wrapped her arms around her ex-stepmother and felt it all over again, this sadness toward the endless passage of time. What had it all meant? Where were any of them headed toward?

"Wow," Karen breathed as she stepped back again. "How have you been, my love?"

Carmella's eyes widened. "Good! Good." She struggled to know what to say next.

Karen lifted Carmella's left hand and said, "I guess no ring on this finger?"

"No."

"And there never was?"

"No."

Karen nodded and dropped Carmella's hand. What was it behind those eyes? Was it pity?

"Well, we should really have dinner together, shouldn't we?" Karen suggested

"Yes, that would be wonderful. There's a lot to catch up on," Carmella agreed.

"What about tonight?" Karen suggested. "I know they're having a dinner here, but I think it's supposed to be rubbish."

Carmella laughed. "I don't mind going tonight."

"Great. I know of a really wonderful Mexican place," Karen suggested. "Nothing like the Mexican food on the Vineyard. I always told Neal how wretched it was."

"Dad was always a sucker for anything on the Vineyard," Carmella agreed. "He never saw anything faulty about it."

Karen collected her eyebrows together over her nose in sudden worry. "Darling, I really was so sorry to hear about his passing."

Carmella's eyes glistened once again. "Yes. It was a surprise."

"It must have been difficult."

"It wasn't easy."

Karen nodded. Her face flattened again. "I'll just finish up here, grab my things from the office, and then we can head out together, huh? Girls' night!"

"Girls' night," Carmella echoed. Her heart pounded with excitement.

Finally, she would get the closure she'd always craved. Finally, she'd be free.

CHAPTER FIVE

KAREN HAD RENTED a car for her stint in the Southwest. She clicked the key fob and pointed it toward a bright white Porsche, and the lights flashed. Carmella struggled to know what to say as she walked alongside this woman, a woman she had once loved like a mother. Was she a stranger now? As she slipped into the front seat, her mind flashed with the final memory she had of Karen just before she'd left Martha's Vineyard. "Don't let Neal and Elsa destroy you," she'd said as her eyes had darkened.

But now, the Southwest sun eased into the soft slumber of twilight, and all the horrors of their yesterdays had no bearing on reality. Karen messed with the stereo and said, "I always love the radio stations in Santa Fe, don't you?" Carmella remembered when she had lived there how she'd marveled at the way her life had shifted so completely from her time on the Vineyard. She had been a completely different person, with different friends, a different closet. Why had she ever left the Southwest? Maybe she could have stayed on there, opened her own acupuncture practice.

She said this to Karen, now. "Sometimes, I wonder why I ever left."

Karen nodded somberly. "I wonder why you did, too. But I guess we'll get to that over some margaritas, huh?"

A wave of Mexican food scents came over them as the door opened. Karen smiled at the hostess, who greeted them and sat them immediately at a booth near the table. Within the first few minutes, they had their first salt-lined margaritas. Karen lifted hers toward Carmella and beamed.

"To us, right?"

Carmella nodded. "To us." She meant it with all her heart.

The sour liquid traced a line down the back of her throat. Karen tapped her tongue against the top of her mouth and then said, "Oh, they really have good fajitas here. Are you hungry?"

Carmella felt it was so strange to hear such a normal question after so much time away. Was she hungry? She had no idea. What did she feel, exactly? At a loss. Maybe that was a better way to put it.

But instead, she just said, "Starving. I haven't eaten anything since I left the airport in Boston."

"Then fill up on these chips," Karen said brightly. "They make their own salsa here. It's divine."

Carmella remembered a long-ago night when she had actually been to this exact same Mexican restaurant. She'd been on a date with a guy she had met at the acupuncture school. It had been strange, one of the first dates of her life, in fact, and she'd spilled that homemade salsa all over the table. Carmella thought about telling this anecdote to Karen but then thought better of it. She didn't want Karen to think she was some idiot.

"I can't believe you're here," Carmella said, just after they finished ordering.

Karen nodded. "And you! The thought didn't even cross my mind."

"But you knew that I came here for school," Carmella pointed out. "We talked about it so much before you left."

"You mean before your father kicked me out of the house," Karen corrected.

Carmella shifted her weight on her chair. Karen's words felt like a strange smack in the face. Almost immediately, Karen fixed her face and lifted her eyebrows and said, "But that's all in the past now, isn't it?" She then took a chip and scooped up a lot of salsa.

"Anyway, this school totally changed my life," Carmella said. "It made me who I am today. And I've really loved being an acupuncturist."

"You've worked at the Katama, have you?"

Carmella nodded. Her smile faltered again.

"I wondered if you'd ever go out on your own," Karen said. "Away from Neal and Elsa. Away from everything you'd ever known."

Carmella swallowed. Karen had the smallest of chip crumbs on her chin, but she still continued to look at Carmella with those intense eyes.

"I remember you so well as a teenager," Karen said then. "You were so sullen."

Carmella's nostrils flared. "I mean, my mother and brother had both—"

At that moment, the waitress arrived with an appetizer. Carmella had forgotten they'd even opted for one. Karen thanked the waitress and then lifted a fork and knife, prepared to dive in.

"Oh, but we shouldn't talk about all that," Carmella tried brightly. "Why don't you tell me what you've been up to?"

"Gosh, there's so much to say," Karen began. "I guess, after the Vineyard, I took some time over in Europe. It was so beautiful to be back. I was in the south of France, mostly before I headed into Spain. By the time I thought about your father again, I'd already mastered the Spanish language and taken a Spanish lover."

Carmella swallowed again. "Wow."

"Yes, but it wasn't meant to last. Nothing good in life is ever meant to last," Karen told her. "In time, I returned to the States. I got married again — to a banker, of all people, and then we divorced about five years ago. Around then, I went to Wisconsin, which is where my sister lives. I have to admit that I like having her around."

Carmella felt the immensity of Karen's life without her. How had Karen done so much during her time away? How had she lived so much while Carmella still felt handicapped in her own life?

"You know, I never really loved the Vineyard," Karen said a few minutes later. "It was so stifling to be trapped on an island like that. Your father wouldn't have ever dreamed of going anywhere else."

"The Lodge was his life," Carmella pointed out.

"Yes, well. I asked him to hire new management so that we could go begin a new life elsewhere," Karen said. "I think both you and Elsa would have had more opportunities if we'd even gone up to Boston or gone to New York. Your father had the money to afford anything. Yet, there you two went off to that silly school in Edgartown. I couldn't understand it. I asked Neal over and over again why he didn't want the best for you. But he just wouldn't leave the island."

These were things Carmella had never known about Neal or about Karen. She wasn't sure she liked to hear them, now.

"That's not to say I didn't enjoy some parts of my time there, of course," Karen continued. "Sailing and swimming. And spending time with you, of course, Carmella."

She said it as though it was expected of her to say it. Carmella found herself not fully believing her.

"But what keeps you there?" Karen asked then. "A boyfriend? You were always so chummy with that boy. What was his name?"

"Cody," Carmella recited.

"Yes. What happened there?"

Carmella furrowed her brow. "He's still on the island. He married someone, but they got divorced."

"He was so in love with you," Karen said. Her words seemed sinister and unkind.

Carmella shook her head. "We're just very good friends."

"Right. I don't think men just have female friends like that, but what do I know? So tell me about Elsa. Of all the people I've met in my life, I swear, she's one of the slimiest," Karen sneered. "She was the ultimate reason Neal broke our marriage off, you know."

Carmella had been terribly resentful toward this very fact. She wasn't so sure about it now.

"Actually, Elsa and I have begun to mend our relationship," Carmella told her.

"Ah. Is that so?" Karen sounded bored with this idea.

"I figured I couldn't stay mad at her forever," Carmella said.

"And she's been through a lot. Aiden died last year and you know how close she was with Dad. She didn't take his death well."

Karen arched an eyebrow. "Well, yes. That all sounds very hard."

Again, she sounded sarcastic. Carmella's heart darkened.

"She has two kids?" Karen asked.

"Three, actually. Cole, Mallory, and Alexie."

"Huh. She got busy, I guess," Karen stated in a tone Carmella didn't like.

"She's a great mom. She's actually a grandmother, now."

"Wow. Time really does pass, doesn't it?"

Their food arrived. Carmella had never been less hungry in her life. She watched as Karen tore into her fajitas and listened as she told another anecdote about another man she'd had an affair with. Carmella had had relations with fewer men than she could count on one hand. It just hadn't happened much for her; she'd allowed it to all pass— all of it.

"Anyway, how did it go after I left?" Karen asked as she scraped her plate clean. "Did your father and Elsa ever get over their anger toward you?"

Carmella allowed her fork to fall to the plate below. She blinked at Karen. "What do you mean?"

"You know. It's why I wanted to take you with me. They never got over your brother and everything that happened. Gosh, it was a tragedy, wasn't it?" Again, she said it all as though it had happened to someone else.

Carmella's throat felt on the verge of closing. In truth, she'd never really gotten over it, not any of it. How could she have? It seemed as though Colton lived on in everything she did; he was in the air and the water and the sands. He was her constant ghost.

"I really didn't mean for any of that to happen," Carmella said softly. Her voice broke. The tears threatened to fall.

"It was a long time ago. But you know, just as well as I do, that they blamed you for all that," Karen continued.

Carmella couldn't contain her tears. They fell and rolled down her cheeks as she stared at Karen in disbelief. She finally reached for a napkin as a sob escaped her throat.

"Carmella, please. Calm down. It was all a long time ago." Karen searched the tables around them to make sure that nobody looked at them too strangely.

But Carmella full-on wept, then. She couldn't keep the tears in. The emotion of seeing Karen again had brought so many memories to the surface. There was no way she could keep it together, no way on earth. She continued to cry as her shoulders shook. "I can't do it. I can't," she said over and over again.

"At least take yourself to the bathroom, Carmella," Karen said pointedly.

Carmella leaped from the table and rushed toward the back of the restaurant. Once inside a stall, she cried louder and harder than she'd cried in years. With Karen there, she again felt the immensity of Elsa and Neal's anger toward her. She could now see her own mother's eyes during those years before the accident. They'd never been allowed any moments of reprieve. They'd never been allowed to come together as a family again.

And Neal had picked Karen to try to bring love and companionship back into his life.

Now, as a forty-two-year-old woman, Carmella fully

understood the horror that Karen had put upon her and Elsa's relationship. She hadn't had any respect for Carmella or for her age or where she was headed or where she'd been. She had been only a pawn — something to link her to Neal's family. She'd wanted their money and not a whole lot else.

What an idiot Carmella had been so long ago. She'd actually gone to the school Karen had gone to. She had actually hoped to become somewhat like her. Now, more than twenty years later, she felt the heaviness of her mistake. "I really messed up," Carmella breathed.

Carmella was grateful that she'd brought her purse from the table. She stepped out from the bathroom and then eased through the tables. Karen was bent down over her phone. She wouldn't notice. Carmella swept out into the evening night, then immediately jumped into a taxi. She prayed she would never see that horrible woman again.

CHAPTER SIX

IN THE BACK of the cab, Carmella's soul threatened to burst from her chest. She placed a hand over her throat and focused on her breath. The taxi driver played an old Pink Floyd song and it reminded her of her father, long ago, when he'd sat on the back porch alone and gazed out across the waves. It was magical and unnerving, the way music could transport you to places you didn't necessarily want to go. In any case, the idea of returning to her hotel room and staring at the wall alone, still hungry and out of her mind, did not please her. She found herself asking the taxi driver about a good dive bar in the area. She needed a drink.

The cab dropped her off at the far end of a busy street and instructed her to walk one block down, then turn left into a side street, where a place called "The Alley Cat" was located under a black overhang. Carmella pressed open the dirty glass door and found herself in a dank, shadowy place. The jukebox played David Bowie, and the bartender had a handlebar mustache and more of that turquoise jewelry. He told her to sit at the bar if she wanted to, and she found a stool toward the side. There, she ordered herself a double whiskey. This, too, had been her father's drink — and Neal was clearly heavy on her mind.

Carmella lifted her phone and considered texting Elsa about what she'd just experienced. But she half-imagined that Elsa wouldn't be pleased at all with Carmella's decision to go out to dinner with Karen, especially since Elsa and Carmella were in the middle of repairing their relationship. Carmella didn't want to start another fight. She slid her phone back into her purse and stared up at the television, which showed a pool tournament.

Carmella wasn't fully aware that she was crying. Her eyes welled up, but she tried to focus all her attention on the pool game that played out on the screen in the corner. It was oddly meditative. The balls scattered every which way across the green field and rolled into the little pockets. The players sauntered around the pool table with a sense of confidence and ownership, the likes of which Carmella was sure she'd never had in her life.

"I've never seen anyone cry over a pool game before." The voice came from her left.

Carmella turned her head slowly. A man had sat two stools away from her — a handsome man, maybe late thirties or early forties. He drank a dark beer and wore a leather jacket with a white t-shirt beneath it. His hair was tousled and his cerulean eyes glittered from the soft light of the various beer advertisement neon lights. He looked at her as no one had looked at her in ages — as though she was an interesting stranger. She knew in her heart she was not.

"Oh. Yeah." Carmella lifted her napkin and dotted it across her cheek, even as another round of tears fell. "I guess it's just been a hard night."

The man glanced up at the TV and said, "Should we call them and tell them how upset you are with them?"

Carmella's lips quivered into a smile. "Do you think they'd take it well?"

"No. I don't think these guys take anything well," the man said. "But it's worth a shot. Aren't you supposed to tell people how you're feeling in this life? Waste of time to live in your own misery."

Carmella couldn't help it; this man was endlessly charming. He lifted two fingers and ordered her another whiskey, as she'd apparently already drank hers, and then asked if he could sit at the stool directly beside her. Loneliness made her nod her head yes.

He lifted his beer, and she clinked her new whiskey with his glass. Again, her eyes found his hungrily.

"You're not from around here, are you?" the man asked.

Carmella shook her head. "I came here for school about twenty years ago, but this is my first time back."

"Wow. What was it like to live here?"

Carmella forced her mind back to those beautiful, sunny memories. "Hot, I guess, but calming. I had gone through a lot the decade before, and I needed an escape, so this was the place."

"You ran to the desert to get away from it all," he said.

"Something like that."

He stuck a hand out between them and introduced himself. "I'm Cal."

"Cal. What's that short for?"

"Calvin. But isn't that awful? My mother had a vendetta against me."

Carmella, who'd always sensed that her mother actually had had a vendetta against her, struggled to laugh at the joke. Still, her smile remained.

"I'm Carmella," she replied. "It's nice to meet you."

"I'm not from around here either, you know," Cal said. "I'm here on a work trip."

"Oh? What do you do?"

"I'm a journalist," he explained. "But kind of a trashy one, sometimes. You have to go where the work takes you. But I'll head out of here in a few weeks, I guess. I'm so ready to be back by the water."

Carmella nodded. "I thought I would be here a few weeks, but something just happened. And I think I might get on the first flight back to Martha's Vineyard."

"Martha's Vineyard! Now, that's a place I've never been," Cal said. "Tell me about it. You grew up there?"

Carmella nodded. She recited the everyday rhetoric about the sand and the water and the sailing and the woods and watched his eyes light up.

"It sounds like heaven," Cal said.

Carmella had to admit, from an outside perspective, it really did sound like heaven.

"But why are you headed back so soon? And what are you here for?" Cal asked.

Carmella buzzed her lips. She wasn't exactly keen on the idea of laying out her dirty laundry in front of a stranger, but she rationalized that she'd never see this guy again.

"I came here for an acupuncture clinic. My ex-stepmother happened to be one of the guest speakers, and we decided to go out to dinner. But a lot of stuff happened between us back in the day and she started dragging up these old memories. I got so upset. She really made me and my sister turn on one another. We're in the middle of fixing all that damage, so seeing her wasn't exactly good timing."

"Is there such a thing as good timing?"

"I don't know. Probably not," Carmella agreed.

"But this sounds fascinating. I'm so used to writing silly celebrity gossip. But this is real family drama. The height of what keeps us together also tears us apart," Cal said.

Carmella nodded. "I couldn't agree more."

Carmella sipped her whiskey again and began to tell him more: more about the Katama Lodge, about her father, about her mother, about her brother's death. She told him that her mother never really forgave her for Colton's accident. "And then, before I knew it, she was dead, too."

Cal's eyes were soft with sadness. As she explained a tiny bit about what had happened with Karen and how busted up she'd been when Karen had left her behind, he reached a hand across the bar and splayed it over hers. "That sounds tremendously difficult. No wonder you wanted to get away."

"All these years, I've half thought, that what if Karen had stuck around? She was the only mother figure I loved once my real mother had passed away. I don't think I really realized how much I felt abandoned by her. And now, all she told me is how good she's been over the past few decades. She's been absolutely great, and I've felt like a dried-up piece of trash."

Cal chuckled. "You're funny. You don't have to be funny about this, but — you're funny."

Carmella shrugged and grinned wider. "I guess it's true what they say. Humor is the universal band-aide."

Cal allowed a moment of silence to pass. On the TV screen, a large man performed an insane pool trick, one that sent three balls to their deaths. Carmella imagined she would never be half as good as that at anything.

"It's strange, isn't it? As teenagers, we really believe that adults know everything. But then when we get older, we discover that nobody knows anything," Cal said.

"Yeah. This was exactly the emotion I had at the restaurant tonight with Karen," Carmella affirmed. "Like all these years, I've imagined she would be able to say the exact thing I needed to hear for me to get over all that pain. But instead, she's just a person, living her own life and hardly thinking about me at all."

Cal nodded. He ordered them another round and then blinked those beautiful eyes toward her. "Tell me more about this Lodge, though. I've heard of it before. It's kind of famous with celebrities?"

"Yeah, a little bit. We have a whole range of women coming from all walks of life. They come for healing, wellness and relaxation, and then they blog about it on their various social media channels. To be honest, I can poke fun at them all day, but I actually do believe in what the Lodge does. There's a reason I've worked there for so many years and a reason why so many return year after year."

"I can imagine. It must be really special, knowing you're helping people," Cal said, leaning into the bar.

"It really is. Especially when I really felt that I couldn't help myself," Carmella offered.

The conversation continued on deep into the night. Carmella

occasionally questioned it — why it was so easy to speak with this man, but she soon laid those fears to rest and fell into the soft beauty of his eyes. When was the last time she'd flirted? It wasn't like this was any kind of date. It was just two people at the bar getting to know one another. It was harmless and she'd never see him again anyway.

Still. How beautiful? How wonderful? How right?

Carmella and Cal stumbled out into the dark night. Carmella could sense it in his eyes that he wanted to invite her back to wherever he was staying. But Carmella felt hesitation. She wasn't exactly keen on one-night stands, especially because she felt so inexperienced and she didn't want anything to happen after the bar to taint the beautiful evening they'd had.

"I'll grab a taxi back to my hotel," she said, her words slurred.

He looked palpably disappointed. But he nodded and just said, "It's been such a pleasure to meet you, Carmella." He then leaned down and kissed her gently on her right cheek. "I wish you well."

"You too." Carmella ducked into the back of the cab and focused her eyes ahead. She felt that if she looked back and watched him as he departed from her life forever, her heart might break.

People came into your life for a reason — even for only a few hours. She genuinely felt that Cal had entered her life to save her night. Somehow, it had given her purpose. Somehow, it had made her strong.

CHAPTER SEVEN

CARMELLA STAYED at the hotel the following day in a state of hangover gloominess. She received a call from one of the acupuncturist teachers at the clinic, asking if she planned to show up for any of the classes. She didn't answer and just let the call go to her voicemail. After she listened to it, she promptly deleted it. She couldn't very well show her face there and see Karen again. She felt defeated.

Around three in the afternoon, she booked a flight back to Boston for the following day. She texted Elsa with her plans without context.

ELSA: Are you sure? Did something happen?

CARMELLA: I just want to get back to my clients. I'm already getting so many requests for the next few weeks. I don't want to let anyone down.

ELSA: Mallory and I have decided to pick you up. See you tomorrow? Four?

CARMELLA: It's a date.

Carmella couldn't sleep that night. She wasn't sure if this was what failure felt like or if this was what it meant to take charge of your life. She rose early, before the first heat of the day, and jogged around the city. She expected to feel something as she passed all these familiar sights. Instead, her heart ached to see her home again.

By some grace of God, Carmella managed to sleep on the plane. The wheels touched down on the runway at three-thirty, and her eyes burst open. The older woman beside her chuckled and said, "I wondered if you'd ever get up! I thought I might have to wake you like the dead."

Carmella gathered her suitcase and watched for Elsa's car outside. Elsa was forever prompt, and she pulled up right at four, just as she'd said. Mallory slipped into the back seat alongside her son, Zachery, who slept somberly, with his brows furrowed. Carmella's heart leaped at the sight of the three of them. This was real love, and she wanted to be a part of it— forever.

"How was the Southwest?" Mallory asked as Elsa drove the car away from the airport.

"Hot," Carmella answered. "And I just wanted to be back by the water."

"I can imagine," Mallory affirmed. "We would have missed you too much, anyway."

When they arrived back to Nancy and Elsa's house, the house in which Carmella had been raised, Nancy stepped out onto the porch and waved a hand in welcome.

"I forgot to tell you. We're having a barbecue tonight," Elsa said as she shut the engine off. "I hope that's okay?"

"More than okay," Carmella replied. In truth, she was starving. Food hadn't been an essential part of the past few days. "What can I help with?"

Soon after, Carmella found herself carving into the belly of a watermelon. Janine and her daughters stepped in and out of the kitchen in a flurry of conversation and gossip. The eldest, Maggie, would be married soon. An autumn wedding and it seemed there was always a new thing to say about it. As Carmella loaded a platter of sliced watermelon, Janine's new boyfriend, Henry, appeared in the kitchen with a bottle of natural wine. He greeted everyone sheepishly and then dotted a kiss on Janine's cheek. She blushed and grinned at once, like a teenager.

"Who else can we expect?" Nancy asked as she prepared a platter of vegetables. "Elsa, is Bruce stopping by?"

"He is!" she called from the back porch. "He should be here any minute."

"Wonderful," Nancy beamed. She then side-eyed Carmella and added, "I have to admit. I like that Bruce character."

"Me too," Carmella said, although she hadn't spoken to him much. He was an attorney at the Law Offices of Sheridan and Sheridan, the place Susan Sheridan had started up earlier in the spring. He was incredibly handsome and responsible and caring — all the things Carmella wanted in a partner for her sister. Even still, it was strange for Carmella to see Elsa with anyone who wasn't Aiden. Despite her frequent annoyance at their happiness, Carmella had always honored them as perfect. When Aiden had died, Carmella had cried privately for days, as she hadn't wanted Elsa to know the depths of her sorrow for a man Elsa had loved so dearly.

In essence, Carmella had always felt that Aiden understood her in a way that Elsa never could.

For dinner, Nancy made Caesar salad, barbecue chicken and homemade French fries. Carmella sat at the far end of the long porch table with her glass of chardonnay and dipped her head back as the conversation rolled around her.

"Mom, the city is just so hot right now," Alyssa said to Janine. "I was telling Maggie that we should just stay here and swim until autumn comes."

"You know that everyone is welcome in this big house," Nancy affirmed. "We like the chaos. Don't we, Janine? It was only us for so many years, and now we have a community."

"It's more like our own little clan, isn't it?" Janine teased.

Maggie and Alyssa whooped with laughter. At that moment, baby Zachery scrunched his face up and started wailing. Mallory leaped up to go care for him, saying that he needed a changing. Bruce lifted a hand over Elsa's on the table and caught her eye while Henry began to talk about the documentary he'd continued to film that summer, all about the history of Martha's Vineyard.

Nancy turned to find Carmella's gaze. "Tell me. How was it, really out west?"

Carmella swallowed. She wasn't sure how honest she could be with Nancy, as they'd never had the strongest of relationships. "When I got there, I just realized I was needed here more."

"That makes sense. I understand that feeling of displacement," Nancy offered. "When you're so sure that if you can be anywhere else, you'll be happier. But once you get there, you just feel like you don't fit in."

"Something like that. Yeah," Carmella affirmed.

"But Elsa says you already have several appointments lined up for the week?" Nancy asked.

"Yes, I do. I'll be at the Lodge bright and early tomorrow," Carmella said.

"Us too," Nancy said, beaming. "I'm doing morning yoga at six. You should come before your first appointment!"

Carmella had never once agreed to a morning yoga session with Nancy. She had always resisted the woman's advances toward friendship and bonding. But now, she found herself nodding. "That sounds nice."

Nancy beamed. "I think you'll really like it. I know you're still young and spry, but that goes south quickly, believe me."

"You're about as healthy as they come, Nancy," Carmella said. "You drank from the fountain of youth, didn't you?"

"Not quite. I never managed to find it on all my travels across the world," Nancy admitted. "But that doesn't mean we can't make some of our own. We can mix it with whiskey, maybe. The way your father would have liked it."

After dinner, Carmella collected the plates, while Elsa and Janine collected the cutlery, bowls and glasses. Together, the three of them piled into the kitchen to clean up. Traditionally, the clean-up was the time when Carmella and Elsa had found new ways to fight and belittle one another. Even now, as Carmella began to load the dishwasher, she felt Elsa's eyes on her. She half expected Elsa to say something about her technique — that maybe, they didn't load the dishwasher that way. What did Carmella know? She'd never had a dishwasher.

Carmella lifted her eyes angrily toward Elsa's. But she found only compassion. Elsa grabbed a box of chocolates from the counter and said, "Bruce brought me these. Want one?"

Carmella washed her hands and selected a piece of orange chocolate. Janine grabbed one, as well. As she bit down, she moaned and said, "That Bruce is off to a good start, isn't he?"

Elsa laughed nervously. From the kitchen, they could hear the booming voices of Bruce and Henry as they discussed a recent sailing expedition from the local sailor, Tommy Gasbarro, who planned to trek back down to the Caribbean, something he'd done frequently.

"I guess somebody has a new friend?" Janine said then.

"We're in big trouble if they gang up on us," Elsa affirmed. "Can you imagine?"

Carmella turned her attention back to the dishes. Her cheeks burned with sudden excitement. After all, hadn't she met a man out west? Wasn't this the kind of story you told your sisters?

"I met this guy at a bar the other night," Carmella said.

Janine and Elsa's eyes widened as they both looked directly at Carmella.

"Are you serious? Tell us more, please!" Elsa cried.

Carmella looked at both of them and chuckled. She had their attention, something she wasn't accustomed to. "He was so handsome. We sat at this dive bar and talked for hours. He was so curious about me. I am not used to that, as you know."

"Not that you couldn't be," Elsa said. "You're one hot lady, sis. Men look at you in the street all the time."

Carmella scoffed. "Don't be ridiculous."

"She's not lying," Janine added. "I notice it, too."

"You're just too closed off," Elsa said.

Carmella gave Elsa a sharp look, one in the style of their previous, darker relationship. Elsa hurriedly mended her words.

"I mean, you're just always so busy with other stuff. They know they can't approach you," she said.

Carmella shrugged. "I just felt totally comfortable with this guy. He was like Cody already, even though we'd just met."

"Ah, Cody. Poor guy," Elsa said.

"Why poor Cody?" Janine asked.

"Because he's loved Carmella for years, and she won't give him the time of day," Elsa teased.

"That's not true. He got married and had a baby, for goodness sake," Carmella clarified.

"People get married and have babies all the time. They don't always fall in love," Elsa returned. "Not the way Cody loves you."

"Whatever," Carmella grumbled, waving a hand in the air to dismiss her sister's comment.

Back on the porch, the family sat together and watched as the waves lapped up across the sands. Nancy poured Carmella another glass of wine, and Carmella felt herself grow more and more comfortable in her strange body. Her thoughts slowed; the anxiety about the Southwest had stalled. Over and over again, her heart told her a story of comfort, of light. There, in the house she knew so well, she'd found some form of peace.

And when the clock ticked toward ten, Nancy said, "You know. That spare bedroom upstairs is always yours, if you want it."

Alyssa and Maggie beamed at her. "Yeah! Stay, Aunt Carmella! The more, the merrier!"

It was strange yet welcoming to hear these two relative

strangers call her "aunt." She formed a smile and nodded. "I guess it would be nice."

"Then, I can wake you up early tomorrow and drag you to yoga with me," Nancy said. "Just like we talked about."

"I definitely want to go, too," Alyssa affirmed.

"Yeah. I'm still working on my perfect wedding body," Maggie slurred as she reached for her glass of wine. "Not doing so well in that department."

"As if. You're a size one," Alyssa pointed out.

Maggie shrugged. "I want to be Paltrow-thin for the wedding. You know that."

Alyssa rolled her eyes and reached for another piece of chocolate. "And I want to be happy for your wedding. Big difference, I guess."

"It's going to be beautiful," Maggie said. Her eyes found Carmella's again, who she'd pegged as the only member of the family who didn't know every piece of information about her approaching wedding. "It's going to be ten times better than any Manhattan socialite wedding. I tried to tell Dad he can't bring Max—"

"Shh..." Alyssa hushed.

Maggie dropped her eyes. She'd nearly brought up Janine's decades-old best friend and now total enemy, Maxine, who their father had left Janine for.

"Anyway, it's going to be wonderful. I can't wait for us all to be together there," Maggie said. "You can keep my crazies at bay."

"Bridezilla, you know we would do anything for you," Alyssa teased.

CHAPTER EIGHT

"YOU'RE KIDDING. KAREN? SERIOUSLY?" Cody sat across from Carmella at the diner with his French fry poised in the air. Beside him, in a high chair, Gretchen smacked a plastic spoon around and gabbed as though Carmella hadn't just revealed one of the strangest and most personal events of her life.

"I'm not." Carmella crossed her arms and continued to avoid her food; the chef's salad she had ordered and promptly decided looked disgusting.

"And you talked to her?"

"We went out to dinner. And then, before the food came, I ran out."

"That's insane."

"I know."

"You really have the worst luck of anyone I know," Cody told her. He gave her a crooked smile as Gretchen whacked her spoon again. Hurriedly, he reached over, grabbed the spoon, then said,

"Remember, Gretch, we're in public. You can practice your drumming at home."

Carmella smiled. She couldn't help it; her heart ballooned with happiness when she saw Cody with his little girl. They were two peas in a pod. She even had his bright green eyes, ones reminiscent of the first leaves of spring.

"So you're letting her start the band?" she asked.

"What can I say? She's a punk at heart," Cody said.

"Tragic. But I'll support them till the end," Carmella said. "Girl power, little lady. Girl power."

Gretchen bounced around in response, then started jabbering about something that had happened earlier on her television show, none of which made sense. Cody took another fry and nibbled at the edge.

"What are you going to do? Are you going to tell Elsa about this?" Cody asked, after Gretchen grew distracted.

"I don't know. I don't know what good it would do. It would just bring up all that old resentment. And we're still trying to work through it. We haven't had a fight in a few weeks, which has to be a record. And I even slept over at their house last night. Like we're all one big happy family."

"The big happy Remington family. I didn't think I'd ever see the day," Cody said.

"Me neither."

A pregnant teenager named Mandy stood at the head of the table and refilled their waters. Carmella kind of knew the girl; she was Amelia Taylor's niece, and Amelia Taylor was one of the heads of city council. The Katama Lodge occasionally had to deal with her for various permits for their events over the years. Amelia was something of a powerhouse on the island, but rumor had it that she'd gotten pregnant around the same time as her niece — both on accident. The thought of it made Carmella anxious. Not the pregnancy, exactly but the fact that people could just move on, build lives, and make such enormous decisions. She felt totally unequipped.

Gretchen ate some of Cody's grilled cheese sandwich, which resulted in a lot of melted cheese across her chin. Cody mopped it up and spoke gently to her. "That's all right, Gretch. You can still eat like the Cookie Monster until you're four."

"What about me?" Carmella asked.

Cody arched an eyebrow. "You can eat however messy you want, as long as you have a few bites of your salad, for gosh sakes."

Carmella laughed. "Fair enough." For Cody, she would. She stabbed her fork through a few pieces of lettuce and nibbled on it slowly. Almost immediately, she felt the slightest bit more awake. Funny what nutrients did to you.

"It's too bad you didn't make it through the clinic, though. I know you were looking forward to it," Cody said.

"Yeah. I just couldn't imagine walking the hallways, thinking all the time that I would run into Karen. I probably would have had some kind of breakdown."

———

AFTER THEY ATE, Cody loaded Gretchen into her buggy, and the three of them headed out toward the boardwalk, which stretched north, toward the lighthouse. The breeze was soft and tender; it curled Carmella's hair over her shoulder and brought tears to her eyes. The contrast to the desert was astounding.

"Gretchen's fever broke last night," Cody said after a few minutes. "Thank goodness. We both slept hard afterward."

"It must be so frightening to see her sick like that."

"It really is," Cody affirmed. "It reminds me of when I was sick as a kid. You're so helpless. You think the world is ending. And in a way, when I see how sad and frightened her eyes are, I feel like the world is ending, too."

"You were always meant to be a dad," Carmella said tenderly.

"Yeah. At least one thing to thank Fiona for, I guess," Cody said thoughtfully. "No matter how many regrets I have about the whole situation, I have to say, Gretchen is worth all the misery."

Carmella paused at the side of the boardwalk and leaned over the fence. Just a few feet away, two sailboats creaked against one another. It had been a long time since Carmella had been out on the water; it had been a long time since she'd felt that level of freedom. Her father had taken her out as a teenager a few times, but often, that had resulted in some kind of fight.

It was one of the greatest dilemmas of Carmella's heart, in fact, that she and her father had never had anything much of a friendship. This had only been exacerbated in the months since his death, as the entire island had mourned him. So often, people stopped her at the store or on one of her runs to tell her how much Neal had meant to them. She never knew what to say.

"Karen remembered you," Carmella said then.

Cody stood up alongside her, the buggy to his left. "Really? That's surprising."

"Yeah. She asked if we ever got together," Carmella said with an ironic laugh. "I guess it goes to show that she never really got me."

"Oh." Cody's voice seemed suddenly faraway. "Right. Yeah."

"She only ever saw me how she wanted to see me. And I should have always known that, especially since she didn't even try to keep in contact with me after she left. We were so close, you know? I thought I could talk to her about anything. But in the end, it's more than twenty years later, and you're just there at a Mexican restaurant, and you're basically strangers. And you're wondering where the time went."

"Yeah." Cody shook his head and then glanced down at Gretchen, who'd begun to sleep in the shadow beneath the overhang on her buggy. "I hope me and Gretch are friends."

"How could you not be?" Carmella asked. "I feel like you already are."

"It's true that when she was a baby and couldn't talk, I would just tell her anything I wanted to," Cody said mischievously. "Almost everything. She was my confidant, and it made it all the better because she couldn't speak and wouldn't remember. Times changed, though."

"You hope she doesn't remember. Who knows? She could have built up a big list of blackmail items."

"That's true. Shoot. Guess I shouldn't have told her about that murder I committed."

"And now you've told me," Carmella said with a heavy sigh. "I guess I'll keep the secret to myself, but only because I don't know who else will eat with me at the diner."

"It's true. Others have grown out of the diner and moved on to adult restaurants. Personally, I can't imagine," Cody teased.

"Didn't you and Fiona always go to that Italian place?"

"Yeah. She loved it. We got into so many arguments there. I think the restaurant considered paying us to come back for more arguments because it was kind of like a performance for the other diners," Cody said. "Phew. My anxiety is hardly palpable, now that I really only see her to pick up and drop off Gretchen."

"What a relief."

Eventually, they wandered back toward Cody's car. Cody asked Carmella if she wanted to come back to his place to eat snacks, have some wine, and watch a movie. Carmella hesitated and then declined his invitation. She hadn't been to her apartment in a few days, and she craved a few moments alone.

"But I'll see you later?" she said.

"Of course. We always have later," Cody said with a wink.

Carmella returned to her apartment and sat at the kitchen table, which featured only one chair, which was all she really needed, as she didn't frequently have people over. She poured herself a glass of wine and then grabbed her computer, where she headed straight for the social media page of the acupuncturist clinic over in Santa Fe.

There were one hundred and forty-three photos posted from the previous two days at the event. Three of those photos were of Karen. Beneath one of the photos were the words: Karen Brosnahan is one of our top instructors at this year's acupuncturist clinic. She brings decades of knowledge, compassion, and wellness to our clinic here in Santa Fe.

"Good grief," Carmella breathed.

She thought about contacting Karen after she spotted her email on the website of the clinic. But what would she say? "Thanks for showing me that my love for you was always wasted." Or, "Thanks for proving me wrong about you all those years," or, "Hope you enjoyed that homemade salsa!"

But none of it would have done anything. Carmella heaved a sigh and checked her phone. Elsa had sent her a photograph of herself, Mallory, Zachery, and Nancy, over at the house.

ELSA: Come over if you want to!

ELSA: :)

Carmella puffed out her cheeks. She assessed the empty space around her, the calendar that hung on the wall without a single note of a plan upon it, and the empty fridge. She headed over to her closet, grabbed a sweatshirt, and then marched out to her car. Her life had always had very, very little in it, but Elsa had extended an olive branch. And Carmella planned to take it and hold onto it forever.

CHAPTER NINE

IT WAS a rare thing for Carmella to find herself with Zachery in her arms. She could count the number of times on one hand. Yet here, now, as Mallory rushed upstairs to fetch a fresh towel and Elsa flipped pancakes at the stove, Carmella held baby Zachery clumsily off to the side of her body. She prayed Elsa wouldn't look at her and call her out on how little experience she had with babies.

It was Saturday morning. Nancy planned to return from a morning yoga session at the Lodge in about twenty minutes, and Elsa had suggested pancakes and a girls' breakfast. Janine was up at the Lodge as well and probably wouldn't be able to get away. "She works really hard," Elsa said now, of Janine. "But it's good. Dad would have loved how committed she is to the clients."

When Elsa did turn around to catch sight of Carmella and Zachery together, she grinned broadly. "You two really do look alike."

Carmella was surprised. "Really?"

"Yes. I can see the similarity in the eyes. Yours are green and his are blue, but there's something about their shape."

"I don't even know what he is to me. If he's your grandson, and I'm your sister..."

Elsa shrugged. "Great Aunt, I guess?"

"Wow. Sounds very... old. I remember some of our great aunts from back in the day. Their houses always smelled like moldy food and they always gave us those tiny orange candies, remember?"

Elsa scrunched her nose. "I can't believe you remember that. I think our last great aunt died when you were, what, four? Colton was three, and I remember it really well because he choked on one of those candies. Mom totally freaked out on Great Aunt Mona for putting him in danger."

Carmella vaguely remembered this. Her mind had held onto the horrible coughing and retching noises that her brother had made as their mother had strained to get the candy from his throat.

Elsa carried the platter of blueberry pancakes out to the back porch. Carmella marveled at her ability to just bring up Colton's name like that. Was this one of their first steps toward healing? As Carmella headed onto the porch, she felt this urgent desire to ask Elsa what she thought about all of this — about their brewing new relationship as "sisters who actually got along." But the question seemed too heavy. And maybe that's how you got through difficult things: you pretended they didn't exist until they went away on their own?

Was that possible?

Nancy appeared on the porch a few minutes later. She seemed a bustling ball of energy. She stretched her arms over her head, squeezed her eyes shut, then pronounced morning yoga as the only medicine she needed. "It keeps me young. And at fifty-nine, that's all I need from anything," she chirped.

Carmella laughed. She then lifted Zachery into his high-chair as Mallory returned to the porch. In recent days, Carmella hadn't seen Mallory's on-again, off-again fiancé, Lucas, at all, and she wondered what was happening with all of that. Again, Carmella questioned how Mallory, at twenty-four, could possibly know she wanted to spend the rest of her life with anyone. But then again, when did anyone come to this conclusion at all?

They ate the pancakes. Elsa told a story about Bruce coming by the Lodge the previous day. "He begged me to hide him away. Apparently, Susan Sheridan took on too many cases, and they're so bogged down with work that Bruce can't see the light of day."

"Didn't she just get married?" Nancy asked.

"She did. To her high school sweetheart," Elsa affirmed. "Scott Frampton. You remember all that drama with his brother?"

"Yes. I have to say. Your father never trusted Chuck. When it came out that he stole all that money from the good people of this island, he just shook his head," Nancy affirmed.

As they piled up the sticky plates, Nancy announced that she had plans for them that day. "The attic has been a mess for years. I always threatened Neal that I would clean the whole thing out. He told me we would get to it one day — and then he went and died and left me with a mess on my hands."

"That's our classic Dad. He always knew how to get out of work he didn't want to do," Carmella teased.

"The man was a terrific worker in almost every respect, but he was a pack rat, too," Nancy added. "But if the three of us attack that attic, maybe we can make something of it. Right now, it feels like it's the same state as my mind up there— messy, chaotic, and all dating back about forty years ago."

Carmella hadn't been in the attic since her teenage years. It was musty and sinister and heavy with dark foreboding shadows that threatened to break her renewed shell. Nancy drew open one of the windows, which lined the very top of the house, and a steady stream of sunlight burst through.

They decided to split up in order to conquer the mess faster. Elsa burrowed herself in the corner while Carmella headed for a stack of boxes, most of which contained old books. Downstairs, there was the soft cry of Zachery, then Mallory's murmur, telling him it would all be all right.

Most of the books within Carmella's pile were crime thrillers. Her father had loved them; he'd read two per week, many of which had similar synopses and similar characters. She had asked him once why he didn't branch out to other genres, and he had basically insinuated that there was no reason to read a book that wasn't a crime novel. She told this to Elsa then, and Elsa burst into laughter.

"He was obsessed. Remember how Mom always picked fun at him and said he wanted to be a detective?" Elsa asked.

"Kind of..." In truth, Carmella didn't remember that at all. So much of her childhood was shadowed with trauma. Had she forgotten all of the good times?

A few minutes after Carmella had gathered the boxes of books on the second floor, beneath the attic entrance, Elsa hollered for her to come quickly. Carmella ambled back into the attic to find Elsa in front of a large trunk. Elsa's face was stricken.

"What is it?" Carmella asked.

Nancy stepped out of her corner and peered into the trunk along with them. There, at the top of the pile of things, was an old sweatshirt meant for a little boy. On the front, read *SPIDERMAN*. Memories washed over Carmella. This had been Colton's sweatshirt. He had worn it non-stop when he'd been six, seven, and eight years old. Their father had suggested that because he didn't wash it enough, that soon enough, Colton himself would be able to walk up walls.

"What else is in there?" Carmella breathed, trying to keep the lump forming in her throat at bay.

Elsa removed the sweatshirt gently to get to the stuff beneath. Letters, drawings, old toys, more clothes — it was an entire trunk set aside for the memory of Colton. Carmella dropped to her knees as her emotions took over. Her memories were on fire. This was a world she'd known so well. The tiny dinosaurs which she had played with herself, as she'd been only one year older than Colton. The clothing, much of which had been hers before it had been passed down to Colton — unisex stuff, like jean overalls and plaid shirts. Carmella inhaled, hoping to find some semblance of Colton's scent, but it had been too long.

"Do you remember this doll?" Elsa asked. She lifted the baby doll from the base of the trunk and pointed its face toward Carmella's.

"Oh gosh. Yes. Colton was obsessed with it."

"We could never figure out if it was a girl or a boy," Elsa commented as she pushed the hair away from the doll's face.

"And Colton said it didn't matter because he was the baby's father and he would care for it no matter what," Carmella agreed.

"What a kind little boy," Nancy breathed.

"He really was. He was so patient, quiet, and loving," Elsa murmured softly.

"We only had a few fights that I remember," Carmella said. "I remember once, he messed up the hair of one of my Barbie dolls, and I totally freaked out."

"You did! You screamed in the next room, and I came running and then told you how much it didn't matter," Elsa said.

"I could never understand why you never thought it was a big deal! They were like my children."

"I know. It must have been so traumatic for you. But I was already, what, thirteen? Nothing like that mattered to me anymore."

"You grew up so fast," Carmella noted.

"So did you."

"I guess we had to, after the accident," Carmella murmured, casting her eyes back down to his Spiderman shirt.

A moment later, Carmella found a stack of papers at the bottom of the trunk and lifted them. At the bottom was a drawing Colton had made with thick crayons. Maybe an outsider would have thought the drawing was just some blobs, but Carmella knew differently. It was three figures — Elsa, Carmella, and Colton: the three musketeers.

"I had no idea they set aside this whole trunk for his memories," Carmella replied, perplexed. The paper shook in her hands.

"I'm so glad they did, though," Elsa whispered.

Carmella swallowed the lump in her throat. Her thoughts raced. "Mom wouldn't look at me those last few years. I just — I can feel all that now, and..."

Elsa gave her a sharp look. "What are you talking about?"

Carmella dropped her eyes to the ground. "Mom. The accident. You know."

Nancy dropped back the slightest bit. The air had shifted. Carmella had said the wrong thing, yet again.

"I don't think you know what you're saying," Elsa said pointedly.

Carmella shrugged and placed the stack of papers back in the trunk. What Elsa had said stung, but it gave more fire to the flames of Carmella's near-constant fear: that she was misunderstood and always would be misunderstood.

"Well. It's so painful to know I'll never get to know your little brother," Nancy lamented, an attempt to smooth things over.

"He was really the best," Elsa said.

Again, Carmella's heart felt squeezed with sorrow. It had been her fault. It had all been her fault.

She stood up, suddenly dizzy and said she wanted to grab a glass of water. She headed down the stairs and wandered toward the kitchen, where she fell against the counter. Inhale, exhale. Inhale, exhale.

It was true what Elsa said: that nobody had ever verbally said she was to blame for the death of Colton. But Carmella had felt it in everything that had happened in the years afterward. Words never had to be spoken; she could feel it in her bones. And even Karen had said it, over dinner — that Neal and Elsa treated Carmella like a second-class citizen in her own home.

Or had that all been in her head?

Gosh, it was too difficult to see through the dense years behind her. It was difficult to fully know what was real and what was imagined, as she'd built up her entire identity around the past.

Elsa appeared in the doorway. Her voice was bright as she suggested that they open a bottle of white wine and take a break from the attic. Carmella forced herself to nod and smile, but she felt strangely battered and bruised. Would she and Elsa ever actually overcome everything that happened? Or would Elsa always brush it all away and tell Carmella she was wrong to have the feelings she did?

In any case, when Carmella arrived home that night, she did something she'd never done before: she searched the internet for local therapists and prayed that somehow, someway, she would find a way through the cloud of grief and guilt in her mind.

It was the first step toward something. And when she texted Cody about it, he texted:

CODY: I am so glad you're watching out for yourself for a change.

CODY: So, so glad.

CODY: Life is a messy thing, and none of us make it out of it alive without self-care. But it's better to do what we can, while we're here, to make ourselves happy. To make ourselves feel love.

CHAPTER TEN

THE FIRST THERAPY session went less than stellar, to say the least. Carmella stood in the splendor of the sun afterward and considered some of the words she'd said, along with what the therapist had said in return.

"Have you considered telling your sister some of these feelings?"

"Have you considered the fact that your sister doesn't know all the pain she and your father and mother caused you?"

"Is it possible that some of this is all in your head? People can only really know things about you that you share with them. We're all in our heads, all the time. We're all living out our own personal stories. We have to let people in."

But Carmella was resistant. She couldn't imagine saying anything like this to Elsa. It felt accusatory. They were on the mend, weren't they? They were finally trying again. It had to be enough.

When Carmella returned to the Katama Lodge for another round of appointments, she found the place in a state of chaos. Mallory stood at the desk with her hair all mussed, as though she had tried to tug it out of an elastic but only half succeeded. Elsa burst past, locked eyes with Carmella and said, "We have a crazy situation incoming."

"What's up?"

Elsa beckoned for Carmella to enter her office. She slammed the door closed and exhaled soundly. Carmella half-considered coming out with what she'd just done — gone to therapy for the first time, but then thought better of it. This was clearly not the right time.

"You know that actress? Helen Skarsgaard?"

"Yes, what about her?"

"Well, she's just contacted us about coming to stay at the Lodge," Elsa blurted out in a panic.

Carmella's eyebrows went skyward. "Wow. That's huge."

"We haven't had a big celebrity like that at the Lodge in decades," Elsa said. "It's always such a mess when things like this happen. And Helen is especially difficult because she always brings in buckets of paparazzi. We have to hire new security. We have to be on guard. She just went through that huge divorce. I'm sure you read about it in the tabloids?"

"I saw something about it," Carmella admitted. "She was married to that politician, right?"

"Yes, from France," Elsa muttered. "And now, apparently, she's a wreck and she wants all the healing and comfort we can give her. In the meantime, our mental health is about to go down like a battleship."

Carmella could have chuckled at that. After all, her mental health felt about as lackluster as ever. How could it possibly go south even more?

"Where is she staying?"

"We're going to put her in the largest cabin by the water," Elsa replied, tucking a strand of hair behind her ear continuing to shuffle through paperwork on her desk. "It's the best one. Nicole Kidman stayed there in the '90s and said it was a dream come true. Hopefully, Helen will feel the same? Oh, and we've already begun to organize her schedule— massages, sauna time and plenty of meetings with Janine, who's already planning her dietary schedule for the week. But what worries me most is the paparazzi. I don't want Helen to have a difficult time of it, and I really don't want the other guests to be affected. I just keep thinking about all of them running through the woods around the property, trying to catch a glimpse of Helen. It'll be a nightmare."

"It's going to be fine. Think positive," Carmella affirmed, although she wasn't sure she really believed in the concept at all.

Over the next few days, Elsa, Carmella, Nancy, Janine, and Mallory spent ten-hour days at the Lodge to ensure everything was fully prepared for the incoming celebrity. More staff members were hired and prepped; they had several meetings per day to ensure that security was in check. And by the time Wednesday, the day of the reckoning, arrived, they all admitted that they were about as ready as they ever would be.

They sent along one of their drivers, along with two security guards, to the nearby airport, where Helen's private jet landed just past two. Carmella stood out on the back porch of the Lodge and watched the road like a hawk. Sure enough, even before Helen arrived, several dark vehicles — assuredly filled with tabloid journalists lined the roads. She spoke with their security guards to ensure they headed out to chase them off.

But they would be back. They were like insects after their next meal.

When the Katama Lodge vehicle arrived back with Helen inside, the security guards lined her on either side and marched her toward the foyer. As they walked, three tabloid journalists rushed toward them with cameras flashing. Three other security guards ran from the side of the Katama Lodge and blocked their path and their cameras. They backed off, grinning wildly like hyenas.

Carmella headed into the side entrance and then appeared at the foyer desk alongside Mallory. Mallory shook with excitement as Helen entered. It was strange to see this woman off the large cinema screens. There, in person, she looked fresh and bright, with porcelain skin and blonde, bouncy curls. She wore massive sunglasses, despite the overcast nature of the day, and she wore an oversized body suit, which made her look all the more slender and skeletal. If Carmella had to guess, she'd lost a bit of weight in the wake of her separation and approaching divorce.

Helen's smile was slight. She didn't remove her sunglasses as she greeted Mallory. Mallory placed a key in her outstretched palm as Helen asked, "And you plan to have security around my cabin at all times, correct?"

"That's right, ma'am," Mallory replied. "We've committed ourselves to your health, wellness, and safety, 24/7, Ms. Skarsgaard."

"Thank you," Helen breathed a sigh of relief. "It means so much to hear you say that."

The security guards led Helen off to the front of the Lodge, where a trail led her to the seclusion of her cabin. Carmella and Mallory made heavy eye contact and then exhaled in unison.

"Let the games begin," Mallory deadpanned.

"Now I feel like I'm in an episode of Game of Thrones! It's good press for our Lodge, at least," Carmella teased, winking at Mallory.

"Yes. And it's really so incredible that an A-lister celebrity picked our lodge to help her through such a rough time," Mallory said.

"But still, the stress is...."

"Insane," Mallory finished.

LATER THAT AFTERNOON, Carmella finished up with a client and then took a walk toward the kitchen, where she found their chef in a state of panic.

"Everything has to be perfect for Miss Helen," she muttered inwardly. "But I'm missing pine nuts. I can't believe I didn't buy pine nuts? It was right here on the list!"

Carmella didn't have another appointment for the next two hours. "I can run to the grocery store. I don't mind."

The chef looked at her as though she had three heads. "Are you sure?"

"Of course," Carmella replied with a shrug.

"You'd be saving me. I owe you forever."

Carmella laughed inwardly at the drama over some pine nuts. She headed to her office, grabbed her keys, and then slipped into the front seat of her car. As she rushed out of the parking lot, she spotted several more paparazzi members there between the trees. They spoke together in a circle, probably bored out of their minds and wondering what to report back to their magazines since they couldn't get close enough for any good shots.

Carmella drove toward the grocery store just outside of Edgartown. Once in the parking spot, she opened the mirror above the car seat and fixed her eyeliner and mascara, which had grown messy with the heat of the day. She then grabbed her purse and headed into the chill of the air-conditioned store.

Carmella had a number of items to pick up for herself, as well. She grabbed some lemons, an eggplant, some feta cheese and tomatoes, and then headed for the wine shelves, where she clucked her tongue and assessed the wide selection. She'd spent the majority of the week with her family but had decided to spend the day at home to stew in her own thoughts. Her therapist had assigned her to write a letter to her childhood self — a kind of "you don't know this yet, but..." letter, one of forgiveness. She had absolutely no idea how she would conquer that. Her emotions were a tangled mess of knots.

"Carmella?"

The voice rang out from the right. It wasn't such a strange thing to run into people at the grocery store. In fact, you sometimes had to plan for it to ensure you weren't late to your next plan. Carmella blinked away from the French wine selection and found herself facing a very strange sight.

There, all six-foot-three, broad-shouldered with thick dark hair and bright blue eyes, stood Cal — the man she had met all the way in New Mexico about two weeks previous.

Carmella's jaw dropped. Her heart fluttered with a strange mix of emotions. Fear, excitement, and lust. She shook her head and whispered, "What on earth are you doing here?

Cal's smile grew wider. Carmella was sent back to that beautiful night they'd shared together. She had felt immediately comfortable with him in ways she'd never been with Elsa or with her father. She'd told him all the inner aching of her heart. And now, here he was at the grocery store she had been to over a million times, probably.

He laughed. It was maybe the best sound in the world, that laugh.

"I wondered if I'd ever run into you out here," he said.

"Yeah, I mean. The island is small," Carmella admitted. "We all run into each other eventually. Normally, I'm sick of whoever I run into at the grocery store. But here you are."

"And you're decidedly not sick of me?" Cal asked.

"I just think you might be a ghost or something and none of this is real."

Cal pinched his own elbow and shook his head. "I'm no ghost. Not here to haunt you."

"Then, I'll ask again, why are you here?" Carmella lowered her eyebrows with a sudden wave of distrust.

Cal looked uncomfortable. He shifted his weight and then said, "Well, I told you I was a journalist, right?"

"You did."

"And you might have noticed that there are a number of other journalists here?"

Carmella's lips formed a round O. "What a funny coincidence."

"Well, the idea of one of our writers coming out to the Vineyard for Helen's big visit came up in a writer's meeting for the magazine, and I have to admit, I jumped at it," Cal confessed. "You had talked so much about the Vineyard, and I was so tired of the desert."

"Very strange. I don't even know what to say."

Cal shrugged. "I have to admit. I felt like we had a few more things to say to one another. We did talk all night."

Carmella's throat tightened. He'd remembered her fondly; he had wanted more time with her. When had a man ever felt that way about her? She could hardly remember the last time.

"Well, I have to admit that I don't know how close you'll get to Helen," Carmella replied. "We have pretty thick security."

Cal laughed again. "I figured as much, but whatever. My editor sent me out here, and I plan to enjoy the island for all its worth." He paused and then locked eyes with her. "I don't suppose you could show me around?"

Carmella's heart fluttered like a butterfly. "I don't know."

"I'm all alone here, Carm," Cal said. "And you're the only person I know! Just one drink. I'll pay."

Carmella felt her head drop forward into a nod. How could she resist this man?

"Okay. Okay." Her smile widened. "I'd love to. What about tomorrow, after my last appointment?"

"Sounds great." Cal lifted his phone from his pocket and said, "Can I get your number, finally?"

"Of course." Carmella's smile made her cheeks ache.

CHAPTER ELEVEN

CARMELLA RETURNED to the Lodge in a state of panic. When she reached the parking lot, she realized with a funny jolt that she had forgotten to grab the pine nuts, the entire reason she'd gone out in the first place. She grumbled and headed back to the grocery store, where the teller ogled her and said, "This happens all the time, doesn't it?" then laughed. Carmella replied, "I'm just flustered. It's definitely one of those days."

When she arrived back to the lodge, Carmella handed the pine nuts over to the chef, who asked, "What took you so long?" before she shot back toward the stove top, where several pots boiled. Carmella headed back into the dining room, where she almost ran head-first into Elsa. Elsa's eyes were wide with surprise as her hands outstretched to stop her from falling back.

"Whoa, sis. Slow down before you trip and fall." Elsa said, flashing her sister a grin. "Helen just had her first appointment with Janine. Apparently, it went well. But somehow, a cameraman broke into the foyer! Mallory had to block the door before one of the guards could come to take him away. I can't believe it."

"What? That's insane." Carmella prayed that Cal wouldn't go to such measures, or would he? Ultimately, he cared about her as a person and had openly admitted that he'd conned his way to the Vineyard. Maybe he would step back and not fully commit to the story. For her.

"Are you doing okay?" Elsa asked, even as she began to duck away to whatever disaster awaited her next.

Carmella marveled at the heaviness of the answer she wanted to give. That no, she had about a million things on her mind and she really needed to speak to Elsa personally to describe everything, to fight for honesty and truth. But instead, she said, "Oh, fine. I have another appointment to get to. See you later?"

"Okay." Elsa sounded distracted. "See you."

Carmella returned to her apartment at around six-thirty that night. When she checked her phone, she had two messages, one from Cody and one from Cal.

CAL: It was so wonderful to run into you today. I can't wait for tomorrow.

CODY: What are you up to? Want to order pizza?

Carmella changed into her sweatpants and a huge t-shirt and waited for Cody to arrive. The pizza delivery driver headed up the apartment steps just as Cody parked downstairs. Carmella paid the driver and waved to Cody as he walked up.

"I have some news," she said.

"The island has been nuts with news of this celebrity," Cody said. "There were helicopters overhead earlier, circling the Lodge."

"What?" Carmella cried. "That must have been after I left."

"Is it crazy there?" Cody asked. He slid into the only chair in the kitchen and opened up the box of pizza. Extra cheese, sausage, green pepper — it was the recipe they always ordered together, ever since they'd been teenagers.

"Elsa looks on the verge of a mental breakdown. But I guess that's how we've been in the Remington family for a while now, so, nothing so different," Carmella said with an ironic laugh.

Cody arched an eyebrow and splayed two pieces of pizza on his plate, then loaded up one for her, as well. Carmella opened the bottle of red she'd purchased at the store and poured them both hefty glasses. They then headed into the little living area and sat on the floor on either side of the coffee table, as they traditionally did.

"How is therapy going?" Cody asked. He was the only person Carmella had told about her stints with Dr. Clemens.

"Hmm. I'm not sure yet. I feel a bit whiny, just sitting there talking about my problems."

"That's what therapy is," Cody remarked. "I don't think you should feel whiny. Besides, you have a lot more to whine about than most people. I always feel like I'm outside my element when I'm there. Like, oh, boo-hoo, my ex-wife is mean to me."

Carmella laughed. "Come on. It's good that you go and get that stuff off your chest."

"I have noticed a difference," Cody confessed. "And I hope you do, too, eventually."

"Yeah, but she's right about some stuff. Like, I really need to speak with Elsa. I need to find the strength, to be honest. Otherwise, I'll never get over any of this. I'll never find a way to move on."

Cody nodded. "And you really, really deserve to find peace."

Carmella let a moment of silence pass. She chewed her pizza contemplatively and then said, "Something crazy happened today." She then described the run-in with the journalist from the Southwest. Cody's eyes grew enormous.

"That is seriously weird."

"I know," Carmella admitted.

"But you're going to see him? Even though he's a weird tabloid journalist?"

"He's not weird. And I mean, people have to do something to make money, right? Maybe I would agree to a job like this if it meant I could travel so much. Sounds exciting."

"Exhausting is more like it. And invasive," Cody corrected.

"I don't know." Carmella grabbed her computer and looked up Cal's name. A second later, a number of articles appeared. Several were trashy like, the health and fitness regime of Jennifer Lawrence, and what Michael Douglas did "in secret" in the '80s, and "Which Celebrities Have Had Secret Plastic Surgery." But beyond that, there were a number of articles with more insight, like, "What It's Really Like To Live in Alaska Alone." For the article, Cal had actually lived in a cabin beneath the mountains, by himself, for three months.

"He's clearly very smart," Cody admitted as they read the Alaskan article. "His prose is really wonderful."

Carmella's heart ballooned. "Maybe he does all the trashy tabloid stuff so that he has money to do this other stuff, too? The tabloid stuff is cash in hand, and the other stuff is his art."

"Maybe. It's a viable point." Cody shrugged. "I don't know."

"Maybe I can talk to him more about it during our date tomorrow," Carmella said, beaming.

"A date. Wow." Cody clucked his tongue.

"You sound doubtful."

"I just don't know how much I trust this guy. He sounds like he's stalking you."

"I mean, he kind of is. He admitted to it, though."

"So admitting it means that it's okay?"

Carmella laughed nervously. "Nobody has ever given me the time of day before. Just let me have this, okay? I'm sure he'll run off the island the moment he realizes what a mess I am."

"Or he won't. And you'll fall in love and run around with him on all his tabloid adventures," Cody said.

"Sure. If he wants to stalk Mariah Carey through London and take photos of her drinking green smoothies or something, I would be totally fine carrying his camera equipment," Carmella teased.

"You'd give up acupuncture for him?"

"I would give up everything for him," Carmella joked. "I mean, what else am I doing here? Just living out my days alone and working for my dad's business. Big whoop. Not like I have kids or even an ex-husband to go to therapy for."

Cody turned his eyes toward his pizza. He looked nervous somehow, as though he wanted to say something that he kept inside.

"What?" Carmella asked.

"Nothing. Nothing at all." Cody swallowed a sip of wine, then asked, "Do you want to practice how you'll talk to Elsa?"

"With you?"

He shrugged. "Sure."

Carmella placed her tongue at the edge of her teeth. Her heart swelled with anxiety. How could she even put any of this into words? All those years of resentment and sorrow? All her fears of being not good enough to even be a Remington?

"I guess I could begin by telling her that I ran into Karen? And it brought up a lot of trauma for me?"

Cody nodded. "Not a bad way to start."

"My therapist says that that was particularly bad luck."

"And now, you're running into this journalist. You're just running into everyone," Cody said.

"Yeah. Lucky me," Carmella said sarcastically.

"I don't know. Do you believe in fate?" Cody asked. "Sometimes I think about what I thought when Fiona got pregnant, even though we'd already talked about splitting up. At the time, I thought it was God telling me that I needed to stick it out with her. Now, I don't know what it meant. I guess it just meant I was allowed the gift of that beautiful little girl."

"And she really is so beautiful," Carmella said.

"Maybe nothing means anything," Cody continued. "And it's all random and weird. And we have to hold onto the things we care about for dear life until it all fades away."

"This conversation is already getting dark," Carmella said as she tried to laugh.

"Dang. Sorry. I wanted to help you with your Elsa convo and now, it's just turned into my own thing," Cody said, grinning.

"Typical men. Always making it about yourself," Carmella teased.

"Yeah, yeah. I told you I'd go to that women's march with you, remember?"

"Yeah, but we didn't go and we just ate grilled cheese at the diner instead," Carmella pointed out.

"Sure. But we ate grilled cheese in honor of women everywhere," Cody corrected, arching a brow. "And then you played ABBA on the jukebox and talked about how scummy the guys in the band were since they made the women sing the songs they wrote even as they divorced them."

"Yeah. Wow. Men can really act like garbage, can't they?" Carmella held Cody's gaze as they both burst into laughter.

"We try our best," Cody finally said. "But our best just isn't good enough."

"Hear, hear," Carmella said as she lifted her glass of wine.

The best friends continued on into the night. Carmella was careful not to drink too much, as she wanted to save her face from dehydration. After all, despite her teasing with Cody, she was terribly excited and nervous about her date with Cal the following day. She wanted to look and feel her best. She wanted it to mean something. Gosh, how she needed some kind of meaning in her life.

CHAPTER TWELVE

ELSA SAT at the edge of the acupuncture table and muttered about the various things that had gone wrong over the course of the day. Carmella listened as best as she could, despite the fact that her thoughts raced at a thousand miles a minute. Her phone buzzed, and she glanced down to find yet another message from Cal.

CAL: Looking forward to seeing you later :)

Immediately, Carmella dropped the cup of tea she'd been holding. It tumbled to the ground and splashed brown liquid every which way. She shrieked a bit too loudly, and Elsa dropped to her knees with a package of Kleenex and began to dot at the stain.

"Are you okay?" Elsa asked. "I thought I was on edge."

Carmella heaved a sigh. "I don't know what got into me. Guess I'm just clumsy today."

"I feel you. I nearly tripped on my way up the stairs this morning. I feel off-kilter. I can't wait for Helen Skarsgaard to get done with all her therapy and head back to her mansion in LA."

Carmella rose back up and wiped her forehead. She felt dizzy. She longed to tell Elsa about Cal, about therapy, about all of it, but she didn't want to burden her with even more information. Elsa staggered toward the door and said she had another meeting with Jennifer Conrad, who was handling their social media that summer. She heaved another sigh and said, "Good luck with the rest of the day. Will I see you for dinner later?"

"No. I have plans tonight," Carmella told her.

Elsa arched an eyebrow. "What kind of plans?"

Carmella fumbled for a moment and then said, "I have to clean my apartment." The lie was so weak that she nearly laughed at herself.

"You can clean any time. We need to get through this week together," Elsa said.

"I promise. I'll be around tomorrow," Carmella assured her.

"All right. Fine. If I can't entice you with fresh, home-cooked dinners, then I don't think anything will work."

At six-thirty, Carmella checked herself in the mirror, added another layer of lipstick, then headed out into the warmth of the summer evening. It was mid-August, somehow, and already, there was this sinister feeling to the air, a reminder that soon, summer would be only a distant memory. She had to grab onto it and make something of it before it was too late. Gosh, it already felt too late for so many things.

Cal had texted to say he had parked his car along the line of the forest, in a little outcropping from the main road that stretched out toward Katama Lodge. She spotted his rental, then watched as he stepped from the driver's seat. He had seen her in the mirror. He wore a black V-neck and a pair of black jeans, as a direct contrast to all the white and light blue of the ritzy people of Martha's Vineyard. He looked more like a rock star than a tabloid journalist. Carmella reminded herself of the Alaskan article he'd written about the tremendous insight he'd had after three months in the tundra.

"Hi there." His voice was cultured, deep and smooth.

"Hi." By contrast, she sounded so innocent. "Should we walk?"

"Yes. It's a perfect time for a walk," he replied.

They headed back toward the Lodge. Carmella felt clumsy again, as though her legs were too long for her body.

"I had such a great day today, Carmella," he told her, without skipping a beat. "I swam in the sea, walked in the woods and ate the best breakfast ever at this place called the Sunrise Cove Inn Bistro. I liked the place so much that I actually decided to move over there for my stay."

"I know it well," Carmella concurred. "The inn has been on the island for generations."

"That's what the chef said. I talked to him for a while. His name is Zach."

"Yeah! He's great. He caters some of our events at the Lodge," Carmella said.

"What a tight-knit community this all is," Cal said.

"Sometimes it's too tight-knit. Everyone in everyone else's business," Carmella offered.

They stood before the Katama Lodge. Carmella caught sight of a few paparazzi people off to the side, between the trees. The guards eyed them darkly as though they hunted them for sport. They just waved at Carmella.

"Wow. I feel like VIP," Cal said.

"Want to see the inside?" Carmella asked. "I'm kind of proud of the place, to be honest. I know I went on and on about my complicated family problems, but my dad really did create a fantastic space."

"Of course. I'd love to see it. I read more about it online, and I'm very intrigued."

Carmella and Cal stepped through the foyer, where only a guard sat at the desk. Mallory had left to pick up Zachery from Lucas. Carmella waved again and then led Cal into her acupuncturist office, where she showed him her wide selection of needles. He whistled, impressed.

"You're like an artist that tortures people with needles," he said, echoing what Cody had said time and time again.

"And yet, people come over and over again for that torture."

"The grounds look stunning," Cal said as he peered out the window.

"I can show you. Come on." Carmella led him down the hallway and then back out the wide, wrap-around porch, with its immaculate view of the rolling hills, which swept down toward the bright white sands of the beach. Helen's cabin was located about one hundred feet off to the right, but there was no sign of her. Not that Cal would do anything wrong with Carmella there. He had probably decided not to work on the article at all, knowing that this would be an overstep on his part.

"Wow. This beach! It's all yours!" Cal said. He brought out his phone and snapped several photos of it, including one of Carmella, who grinned sheepishly. It was a really rare thing for someone to take Carmella's photograph. She'd probably gone years without any record of her memories.

"When did you start working here again?"

"Right after I got back from the Southwest," she told him. "I never imagined I would be here my entire adult life."

"There are worse places."

She stole a quick glance before replying. "I guess you're right."

He paused for a moment, then slipped out of his shoes and headed for the water line. It seemed so easy for him to fall into this world. Carmella always felt so strained. When the waves lapped up across his toes, he yelped and turned back. His eyes were bright, like a child's, without a care in the world.

"Is it cold?"

"Not really. I will just never get over how good it feels." He then beckoned and said, "Come with me."

Carmella stepped out of her shoes and joined him, careful to keep a distance between their bodies. The water circled her toes and wrapped around her ankles, and she exhaled deeply. All the stress of the day fell off her shoulders. She'd stood right there, with her feet in the water just like this, probably thousands of times. Somehow, with Cal there, it all felt different. She appreciated it more.

After another twenty minutes of the tour, during which Cal was allowed to taste some of the cuisines in the kitchen, Carmella suggested they head back to Edgartown and have a drink along the water.

"You're my guide," Cal stated. "I'll go wherever you go."

Carmella led him to her car and then traced the easy road north and then east. She parked a block away from a beach-side winery and slipped out. Her heart burst wildly in her throat as Cal flashed her a smile. Was this what it meant to fall for someone? Was this exhilaration something that lasted?

They ordered two glasses of wine and sat at a tiny, circular table near the sand. A sailboat swept out across the Bay and headed up toward the large docks. Carmella told Cal more about the island's tremendous sailing history and that she'd gone frequently with her father when she had been younger. "My little brother was a bit scared of the water," Carmella explained, again surprised that she offered information about Colton so easily. But Cal seemed fine with it. He remembered that her brother had passed away and that information regarding him was something to be held up gently.

"We've started to talk about him a bit more," Carmella said softly. "Me and Elsa. I wonder if we'll ever get through some of our personal problems, you know? We've had so many years of hardships."

"Did you tell her about running into your stepmother in the Southwest?"

Carmella arched an eyebrow, again so grateful that this man had remembered something about her. It had been a long time since someone had shown her such goodwill.

"I haven't, no. And I don't fully know why. I don't want to keep secrets from her anymore. It's just that everything is going so well, even though I can't get some of what Karen said out of my head. In some ways, I know that Elsa and my father and mother didn't blame me. They didn't hate me for what happened. But my memories feel so strong. They're so painful. And I remember the looks they would give me without even realizing it. The words they said, to put it frankly— I didn't feel a lot of love, either from myself or my family, for a long, long time."

Cal allowed silence to fill between them. It was a comfortable silence. He stretched a hand out over hers, there on the table, and held her gaze. "It seems to me that you offer enough love for everyone in your life, despite everything that has happened."

Carmella's eyes glistened with tears. "I'm trying to. Every day, I wake up and ask myself what kind of life I want to live — if I have forty, fifty years left. What will that look like? And I guess it looks like rebuilding my relationship with my sister and becoming friends with my new stepmother and healing women and — oh gosh. I'm rambling, aren't I?"

"No. I like hearing it," Cal affirmed.

Slowly, Carmella continued to reveal more and more about herself. She discussed the history of the Katama Lodge in more detail, along with some of the fights she and her father had gotten into throughout her teenage years. Even as the words spilled out, she recognized how toxic the situation had been.

"Gosh, we all needed therapy so bad," she admitted as she laughed softly.

"We all need therapy to some degree," Cal said. "I've been in it for years."

"Really! That's amazing to me. It's always felt like my family wants to cover up all our trauma and hide it from everything or everyone."

"That's a surefire way to make it destroy you in the long run," Cal said.

"That's kind of what my new therapist said. But I don't know how to explain it to Elsa. And really, she's been through so much, too. Losing her husband last year nearly destroyed her."

A few hours later, Carmella and Cal wandered along the water as the sunset smeared its orange color across Katama Bay. Carmella longed to describe this gnawing feeling she felt as summer descended toward autumn. Another year has gone, and what had any of it meant? What had she accomplished?

"I wonder what Helen thinks of all of this," Carmella said then. "I just can't imagine thinking that you could find healing of any kind elsewhere. Like, she actually thought to herself — in the wake of my divorce, I will go to the Katama Lodge and Wellness Spa to heal myself. But she doesn't know that at the Katama Lodge, we're all just about as broken as she is— maybe even more. And we're certainly not half as rich."

Cal chuckled. "I guess it goes to show that money can't buy happiness, huh?"

"You got that right. The jury is no longer out on that. Money has nothing to do with happiness, although it can take the stress away and it can buy good wine."

Carmella drove Cal back to his car outside the Katama Lodge. She parked behind him and walked him to the driver's side, like some kind of high school boyfriend walking his date back home after prom. She stood there before him and lifted her chin in expectation. And when the kiss came, she felt as though she'd been punched in the stomach with feeling.

This was it. This was what she had been waiting for.

When the kiss broke, Cal looked at her in the eye and said, "That was one of the best evenings of my life. Thank you so much for being my guide on this amazing island."

He then got into his car as Carmella stepped back toward hers. She watched him go as her stomach ballooned with the promise of something. Maybe everything in her life was about to change. Maybe, after so many years of heartache, she'd finally found release.

CHAPTER THIRTEEN

THE FOLLOWING MORNING, Carmella stepped into the Lodge as though she had springs on her feet. A renewed bounce that had her in an incredible mood. Mallory lifted her eyes from the front desk, furrowed her brow, and said, "Are you on happy pills? Where can I buy them?" Elsa popped out from her office with a mug of coffee in hand and grinned broadly.

"I guess you had a good night's rest? Was cleaning that therapeutic?"

Carmella blushed and gave her a slight nod. But in a moment, she recalled her hope for more truth between them, and she felt the news of the night before tumble from her lips.

"Actually, I had a date if you really need to know."

Elsa's face opened like a cracked egg. "What are you talking about?"

"This guy — this journalist guy..." Carmella stuttered as she stepped through the hallway. The emotion of it all curled through her arms and her legs and her stomach so that at no time, she felt she had any power over her limbs.

Elsa followed up behind her. "What journalist guy?" she asked brightly. "Carmella Remington, did you go on a date last night and not tell me?"

Carmella paused in the doorway and turned back. She gave her sister a sheepish smile and then nodded. "I don't think I've ever felt like this before."

Elsa shrieked. "Tell me everything!" She wrapped a hand around Carmella's and jumped up and down like a teenager.

Carmella puffed out her cheeks and led Elsa into her office. There, she leaned against the acupuncture table and explained a few elements about Cal. She explained how she'd met him in the Southwest and he had seemingly come here because he was so interested in her. She left out the part about Helen Skarsgaard, and she skipped over all the elements that involved Karen. None of that mattered. She was falling for someone — really, actually falling for him and she was pleased that her sister cared.

"This is incredible," Elsa said softly. "I don't think I've ever seen you so excited about someone before."

"I know! It's crazy, isn't it?"

"It really is." Elsa shook her head at a loss. "When are you seeing him again?"

"I don't know. I mean, we just said goodbye last night. He's staying at the Sunrise Cove."

"Good taste."

"I just — I want to call him right now and lay out all my cards, but that's a little too intense, isn't it?"

"It is," Elsa agreed with a laugh. "Unfortunately."

"Gosh, how does anyone date? I feel like an exposed nerve."

"Just get through today—one hour at a time. You've already taken so many steps forward. It's a beautiful thing, Carmella. It really is. I'm so happy for you."

As Carmella's appointments passed, she found herself checking her phone impatiently. Noon came and went, and she nibbled at a salad from upstairs, staring at the darkness of her screen. Probably, he would text her to say what a good time he'd had, wouldn't he? That was the kind thing to do after a first date.

But by the time the end of her final appointment came, Carmella found herself with a heavy stomachache and endless, stirring confusion. She wandered back toward Elsa's office, where she found Elsa and Janine in conversation about Helen Skarsgaard.

"She won't listen to some of my advice," Janine said sternly. "She has her own ideas about wellness. I just asked her, then why did she come here? Why did she say she wanted to put her trust in us if she's going to rebuke everything I recommend?"

"And what did she say to that?" Elsa asked.

"She said she's paid us enough to do as she pleases, which is right," Janine offered. "I'm just so frustrated with her. I mean, she's put the Lodge in this crazy state of flux. We're surrounded by guards, and the other guests aren't exactly pleased with the situation. It's stressful."

Elsa nodded. "But there's nothing we can do."

"Nope. All we can do is complain and hope she leaves soon," Janine returned.

Elsa turned to catch Carmella's eye. "You haven't had your acupuncturist appointment with Helen yet, have you?"

"No, not yet," Carmella replied, leaning against the door jamb.

"She told me she's scared of needles," Janine said. "I'm trying to fight that. I gave her all the literature about its healing properties, but she's just kind of blasée about the whole thing."

"I guess it makes sense," Carmella said.

Elsa and Janine gave her curious looks.

"What do you mean?"

"That she'd feel so blasée after such a huge breakup," Carmella said. "She probably wanted to use this time here as a band-aide over the gaping wound in her heart, but it's not an immediate fix. Nothing ever is, except time."

After Janine returned to her office for a final appointment, Elsa latched onto Carmella again. "Has he texted?"

Carmella dropped her eyes to the ground. "He hasn't, no."

"What? That's crazy. But I guess it's all a part of the game, isn't it?"

"What game?" Carmella asked. She was frightened to feel tears welling up in her eyes. She couldn't give this relative stranger so much power.

"I don't know. I don't understand any of it. I've only ever dated Aiden and now Bruce. And Bruce is old enough and solid enough not to play games like that," Elsa returned. "But this guy, he's not from here. He probably operates from a different book of dating rules."

"I feel totally ill-equipped to handle this," Carmella breathed.

Elsa smacked her hands together. "The only antidote is a home-cooked meal and a bottle of wine. Are you done for the day? Let's head home."

Elsa insisted on driving Carmella back to the main house. They found Nancy already in the kitchen, stirring up a batch of lemon butter shrimp. She had cracked a bottle of pinot grigio, and within five minutes, Elsa and Carmella had poured themselves glasses and leaned against the counter to chat. Nancy told them about her yoga session with Helen earlier that day. That she'd basically protested everything, Nancy had said and spouted that some guru in India had told her a different way to stretch out.

"I wanted to tell her to just go back to India," Nancy said with a funny smile. "But of course, we have to treat that girl like royalty."

"Did you see that the Lodge was featured in The New York Times?" Elsa asked. "A huge write-up about Helen and her failed marriage and her decision to take a sabbatical here."

"We already had so many requests for stays over the next few months," Nancy said. "It's insane. Normally, we slow down by September, October, but we're totally booked till the first week of December."

Carmella gazed out the window somberly. Her shoulders slumped forward with sorrow. She couldn't feel happiness toward the Katama Lodge and its tremendous success. She continued to trace through the events of the previous evening for some sign that she'd done something wrong.

"Are you okay, Carm?" Elsa came up beside her to stare out the window.

"I'm fine, really."

"She doesn't sound fine," Nancy said from the stove.

"Just some guy," Elsa said. "He really is a stranger. I hope you know that you don't need him..."

"I know. I know." Carmella cleared her throat and then said something even more vulnerable. "I just don't know when you're supposed to trust your gut and when you're supposed to abandon all feeling..."

"I remember asking myself just that when I met your father," Nancy said. Her spoon clanked against the side of the skillet of shrimp as both Elsa and Carmella turned back to watch. "I had been tossed around by men my entire life, it felt like. When this strong, handsome, rich, and wonderful man wanted to spend time with me, I didn't trust it. Not in the slightest."

"And why did you let it happen? How did you find the strength?" Carmella asked.

Nancy lifted the wooden spoon into the air and blinked several times as though she tried to conjure the memory. "I took it one day at a time. And eventually, by the time we got back here and we got together, I realized I trusted him more than any other person in the world."

Mallory arrived home with Zachery and Lucas in tow, and the conversation found room for other things. Janine entered the porch right as they cracked another bottle of wine, heaved a sigh, and said, "I really need a glass." Carmella eased back further in her chair and felt a wave of emotion crash over her. This was home; she'd shared some elements of her emotions about this guy, and they'd welcomed her honesty. This was very new to her. She made a mental note to explain the big step forward to her therapist.

She knew what her therapist would say in return: "But have you talked to Elsa about your feelings about the past thirty years yet?" And she would have to say no, that she was still too afraid. She didn't want to break the delicate glass of their growing sisterly bonding. It was too much.

Carmella fell asleep at the house that night, then forced herself through another two days at the Lodge without any correspondence from Cal. Her heart felt so battered, so bruised. She stared at her phone as though it was about to self-destruct.

Finally, at the end of the third day, Elsa entered her office, placed her hands on her hips, and said, "You know, there's nothing stopping you from making the first move."

This went against everything Carmella understood about dating, which, admittedly, was not much. She blinked at Elsa, totally flabbergasted.

"He won't think I'm pathetic?"

"If he does, then he's not the right guy for you," Elsa quipped.

Carmella lifted her phone and sent a text.

CARMELLA: Hey! How is the island treating you? I would love to meet again before you go.

She then screamed and threw her phone onto the couch along the wall. Elsa laughed and clutched her stomach.

"I swear to God, dating feels like heartburn," Carmella groaned.

"It really sucks," Elsa affirmed.

Carmella placed her hands on her hips and watched her phone over the next fifteen, twenty seconds. And just when she wanted to give up on it, it flashed. When she lifted it, she found a welcoming message from Cal, the man she'd basically obsessed over the previous few days.

"Is it him?" Elsa asked.

"It is."

"Read it!"

Carmella couldn't remember the last time Elsa had shown such interest in her life. She beamed as she read it aloud.

"Carmella, great to hear from you! I'd love to get a

drink. What about tonight? Meet me at the Sunrise Cove?"

Carmella and Elsa screamed in unison and jumped up and down like teenagers. Elsa wrapped Carmella in a hug, then said, "I always knew you'd find happiness, Carmella."

"Don't get ahead of yourself," Carmella told her, even as her heart ballooned three times its size.

But later that night, as Carmella drove over to the Sunrise Cove, she was overcome with a sense of hope. Anything really could happen if you dared to believe in it. She was mending her relationship with her sister; she was finding new ways to laugh and to love. She deserved it. After so long, it was her time.

Cal waited for her at the Sunrise Cove Inn Bistro with a bottle of wine and olives, cheeses and freshly baked bread. He was exceedingly handsome, and he flashed that now slightly familiar smile toward her as she stepped toward him. A blush crept up across her breasts, over her throat and across her cheeks, and she beamed at him as she sat.

"Hi," she said.

"And hello to you."

There was such tension between them. Carmella found herself fumbling for conversation topics. After their first glass of wine, she eventually found herself laughing easily, tumbling through conversation. She made Cal laugh several times, a fact that thrilled her. And when he asked if she wanted to go to his suite for another glass of wine, she nodded slowly, careful to keep her excitement at bay.

They walked through the foyer toward the staircase. A young man stood at the foyer counter — not a Sheridan, as far as Carmella knew, although it was difficult to keep up with the mass numbers of Sheridans. They seemed to come out of the woodwork. He bid them goodnight as they headed up the steps, and Carmella blushed all over again. Was she really going to spend the night? With this guy? At the Sunrise Cove?

Upstairs, Carmella sat at the edge of the suite's couch and poured them both glasses of wine. Cal checked something on his phone and muttered something about his deadline from that day. Carmella breathed a sigh of relief. After all, if he'd had a deadline, then that meant he'd had reason enough not to text her. People were busy—people who weren't her, at least.

"To your deadline," Carmella said as she lifted her glass to clink against his.

"Thank you."

They continued to talk and flirt and banter. Carmella was mesmerized by how comfortable she felt. She could have gazed into his eyes forever.

Eventually, they kissed. Carmella wasn't entirely sure on the details of who kissed who — just that suddenly, his arms were around her and her heart pattered wildly in her chest and she was lost in a sea of lips and the immensity of her feelings.

If this was what living was, she wanted all of it— forever.

CHAPTER FOURTEEN

YEARS BEFORE, when Carmella had been maybe eight or nine, her father had said something that stuck with her. The only constant in this world — the only thing that never changed was change itself. The sentiment had struck her as strange and sad at the time. After all, she'd looked around to see her mother, her brother, her sister, her father, and their dog at the time and asked herself, how could she possibly live any other kind of life?

That morning, Carmella blinked awake and discovered that she'd stretched herself out on the couch in Cal's suite. She was fully clothed, with a large quilt over the top of her, and her makeup remained caked to her face, which was a big no-no, according to Mila Ellis, the woman who owned the esthetician salon. Carmella's head echoed with the severity of her hangover. She groaned inwardly and lifted herself the slightest bit from the couch. At the far end of the room, Cal was tucked away in bed. Light snores rolled out from his throat.

What had happened? Carmella remembered they kissed, then nothing much at that. She guessed she had just fallen asleep, and he'd had the kindness to place the blanket over her and let her dream away into darkness. She was a bit disappointed, but also not. She hadn't fully been ready to go "all the way" with this relative stranger. Besides, if it was real, then what was the rush?

Carmella's purse sat alongside the couch. She reached for it, unzipped it, and then found her phone at the top. The time was eight-thirty — much later than she'd expected. She didn't have an appointment at the Lodge until eleven, but she needed to head back home and get cleaned up. This gave her pause, as well. She didn't want to go back to the chaos of waiting for him to text her again. Plus, there was the horror of imagining what would happen next. Would he leave the island, even after such a beautiful time?

Carmella had several text messages — all from Elsa.

ELSA: Good luck tonight!

ELSA: Thinking about you so much!

And then, just past eleven, Elsa texted:

ELSA: Oh my gosh! I haven't heard from you. Are you still with that guy?

Then, around midnight, she texted:

ELSA: You! Are! Up! To! No! Good!

But then, at eight-oh-seven that morning, Elsa had written another, more sinister message. It had a link to a Boston magazine along with the text:

ELSA: Call me when you leave his place right away.

Carmella furrowed her brow and clicked the link. It sent her to the Boston magazine, where a title flashed before her eyes.

HELEN SKARSGAARD WON'T FIND HEALING AT THE KATAMA LODGE

Then, the sub-headline was as-follows:

The Katama Lodge and Wellness Spa advertise itself as a one-stop-shop for wellness, health and therapy. But in the process, the Lodge buries its own sinister background that is filled with lies, deception, death, and family secrets that lurk beneath its glossy sheen walls.

Carmella bolted to her feet and gaped at the article. The writer, of course, was none other than Cal. As she read through the first few paragraphs, her arms began to shake and her heart pounded so hard in her chest that it threatened to burst free. He'd written about all of it — about Carmella's relationship with her father and mother in the wake of her brother's accident, about Colton and what had happened, and about Elsa, Aiden, Nancy, and Karen. The stuff about Karen was particularly jolting, as he had also talked about Carmella and what she'd said about their relationship

"I first met Carmella Remington in the Southwest. She'd just had an encounter with her ex-stepmother, a woman who had lived with Neal, Elsa, and Carmella Remington over twenty years previous and also worked at the Lodge at the time. Carmella reported that Karen was guarded and dark, yet another black force beneath the heart of the Katama Lodge. Carmella was very upset about her run-in with Karen, as it had brought to the surface a number of traumatic events within Carmella's life with her

father and sister. *'Maybe she's right. Maybe they never really loved me or cared about me after the accident,'* Carmella Remington says. And it's true that when I look at Carmella, the local acupuncturist, I wonder how such a messed-up creature could possibly care for anyone at all.

"Now, it's up to us to ask — is Helen Skarsgaard receiving the best treatment at the Katama Lodge and Wellness Spa? Is this really the answer to her heartache and horror? I heard several times that the security around the Lodge itself wasn't up to snuff and that several tabloid journalists burst past the lines and took photographs of poor Helen as she reckoned with the healing process. If the Katama Lodge can't uphold security above all things, what are they good for?"

The article was probably two thousand words long. It just went on and on. Carmella's jaw dropped lower, her mouth was instantly dry and she felt nauseated. She felt like a trapped animal. She turned her eyes back toward the slumbering man, a total stranger, and the man who'd violated her trust and totally thrown her family and the Lodge under the bus to advance his own career. Oh God, how could she had trusted him?

She had two options. She could run out of the room and never speak to the guy again. Or, she could demand answers. Maybe a different version of Carmella would have run away. But this version stormed up to his bed, placed a hand on his shoulder, and shook him until he woke.

His eyes popped open. He gaped at her. "What the hell?"

Carmella flashed her phone around to show him the article. "I should say the same to you."

Cal rubbed his eyes and groaned. He then slid himself up to lean against the pillows behind him. "I don't know what to tell you. You know that I'm a journalist."

"But you never once told me that I was a part of your damn story."

"Stories fall into your lap like that, and when they do, you have to grab them. It's just part of the business," he said, like it was no big deal.

Carmella seethed. She wanted to throw her phone at his face. "But what about last night? What about our time in the Southwest? What about —"

He shrugged again. "We just talked. I don't know."

"That wasn't just talking. That was so much more than just talking."

He was gaslighting her. This was what that was. She wasn't sure she'd ever had it happen before. It felt like a double-edged sword had penetrated her heart.

"Whatever, Carmella. You're clearly not really—" He gaped at her.

"Clearly not what?" she demanded.

He shrugged. "You know."

"What?"

"Experienced."

Carmella's eyes widened. The truth of it hit her hard. Still, what kind of man actually called her out on this fact? She couldn't believe it.

"You're a disgusting man. You need to get the hell off this island," Carmella fumed.

He just shrugged. "It's a free country, right?"

Carmella could have thrown a million insults into his face, but she held them back. She jumped back toward the couch, grabbed her purse, and headed for the door. As she gripped the doorknob, she turned back and caught his gaze one last time. She was reminded of all the tiny, little pieces of their experiences together — all the times she'd thought, maybe, it was finally her time to fall in love. How stupid she felt. How stupid to trust such beautiful eyes. How stupid to trust the enormity of her hope.

"Goodbye, Carmella," Cal said. He saluted her like some kind of evil soldier and then gave her that crooked grin. "I hope you get out of that prison soon. Thanks for the great content. My editor loved it."

"Go to hell." Carmella stomped into the hallway and slammed the door closed. Tears sprung to her eyes. Hurriedly, she rushed down the staircase, only to discover many of the Sheridans downstairs, all having some kind of boisterous family meeting around the front desk. There was Amanda Harris, Susan's daughter, along with Susan, Audrey Sheridan and her baby, Max, along with Christine and Lola.

Lola recognized Carmella first, lifted a hand, and then waved. Her eyebrows lowered when she realized Carmella's state. Carmella whipped past her, pretending not to have seen her, but Lola rushed out into the bright morning and called her name.

"Carmella Remington! Stop!"

Carmella stood out on the front porch of the Sunrise Cove and waited. Lola appeared alongside her. She wrapped a strand of hair around her ear and tried to lock eyes with Carmella, who refused.

"I read the article this morning."

Carmella knew Lola worked as a journalist. She turned sharp eyes toward her.

"Do you know him?" Carmella breathed.

Lola shook her head. "I've worked for that magazine several times. I just contacted my editor there to see what's up."

Carmella almost looked hopeful for a moment. "Do you think they can take it down?"

"Probably not," Lola told her. "And because it's about Helen Skarsgaard, the readership will be off the charts."

Carmella allowed the first of her tears to fall.

"He's staying at the Sunrise Cove, isn't he? I thought I saw his name on the ledgers."

Carmella nodded.

"Is that where you just came from?"

Carmella nodded again as her face scrunched up with sorrow. Before she knew what she'd done, she placed her forehead on Lola's shoulder and wept. Lola's hands found her shoulders and she held her softly, tenderly.

"I can't imagine facing my sister right now," Carmella said through tears. "It looks like I totally threw the Katama Lodge and our family under the bus. But I thought I was just getting to know someone! Gosh, Lola, I never get to know anyone! And now this happens!"

"He's an awful excuse for a man. Really. This is something, as a journalist, I would never do," Lola said softly. "I hope you know that it isn't your fault. It really isn't. You walked right into a toxic person who took full advantage of the situation without any regard for your feelings or family. Anyone else would have fallen for it, too."

Carmella wasn't sure that she believed Lola; she wasn't sure she could trust anyone right then. She felt completely vulnerable. One thing that was sure was that Lola was the stronghold she needed right then. She walked her over to her car and made sure she got out of the parking lot okay, then waved a hand as Carmella disappeared back toward Edgartown.

This was the day of reckoning. Carmella would have to face her past and her mistakes. And she wasn't fully sure if she was strong enough — especially with this broken heart.

CHAPTER FIFTEEN

CARMELLA STOOD in a catatonic state in her shower as the water streamed over her back. Her hangover had latched to the back of her head; it felt as though craters formed along her skull. In just half an hour, she would have to face her sister, her stepmother, and her stepsister, and it wouldn't be pretty. Was there anywhere in the world she could possibly run to? For years, she had envisioned herself calling Karen and building a new life wherever she was. That door had officially closed and it was now locked for good.

Carmella parked in the lot, grabbed her purse, and stepped out of her car. Toward the edge of the lot, several tabloid journalists had gathered in a circle. Carmella could just barely make out some of the words they spewed.

"How did he get all this info?"

"He must have had someone on the inside?"

"These photos — how did he make it all the way down to her cabin?"

Carmella clenched her eyes shut. She told her heart to calm itself down and she tried her best to breathe. After another moment, she stepped up the walkway to the foyer, then breezed in to find Mallory at the front desk. Her fingers flew hurriedly as she typed across the keyboard. She hardly glanced up. The air was already sinister, dark.

Carmella headed for the hallway. Perhaps she could escape her sister's wrath, get through her appointments for the day, and then return to her bed alone. All she wanted was sleep. But the moment she entered her office, Elsa's shadow darkened her door. She cleared her throat, crossed her arms over her chest, and gave her that look — the very same one she had given her long ago when Carmella had accidentally broken one of Elsa's toys.

"So, you had quite a night last night."

Carmella felt her heart race and a lump form in her throat. She dropped her purse to the acupuncture table and forced herself to find her sister's eyes. Her own welled with tears. She couldn't control her emotions any longer.

"I didn't know," she breathed.

Elsa's face relaxed the slightest bit. "Of course, you didn't know."

"What's that supposed to mean?"

Elsa shrugged. "I mean, you told him everything. All our dirty laundry. It's all out there, now."

Carmella's nostrils flared. She stuttered, then said, "I mean, I think I'm allowed to talk about it. About everything that happened to me."

"Yeah, but not to a journalist, Carm."

"Then who the heck am I supposed to talk to about it? Because it's been pretty clear over the years that you don't want even an ounce of my honesty or how I feel."

Carmella's heart pattered louder. She suddenly felt all the pent-up anger that had been building. It was the hangover, maybe — or maybe it was just the culmination of decade after decade of pain and heartache and feeling excommunicated from her own family.

"Calm down, Carmella."

"No. I don't think I can." Carmella swallowed the lump in her throat. "I didn't mean to put any bad press out there. You know that the Lodge has been my only home over the years. As you've gotten married and had babies and built your life, all I've had is this. And you know, I wouldn't do anything to jeopardize that. At least not on purpose."

"You've made it pretty clear that you never liked our family. That we poisoned you, and therefore, that we're apt to poison every other woman who comes here for 'healing.' You made us look so foolish, Carmella."

"Why is that the worst part of it?" Carmella demanded. "Isn't it maybe worse that I've felt like I've never fit in, on this island, or within our family — ever since everything happened?"

"You blew it so far out of proportion, Carmella," Elsa blared.

At that moment, Carmella's first client for the day appeared at the far end of the hallway. Carmella snapped a finger to her lips and glared at her sister. She no longer felt any of the goodwill she'd brewed in the previous month. Elsa looked like a stranger.

"Let me do the one thing I'm capable of doing," Carmella said pointedly. "Just let me help this woman."

"Before the Lodge has to close because of the article," Elsa said under her breath. "What the hell would Dad say, Carm? After all he's done for us? After all he's built here?"

"Oh right. Great idea to bring Dad into this. You know how he felt about me."

Elsa lowered her eyebrows. "You don't know what you're talking about."

"Hello!" Carmella said to her client, who appeared directly behind Elsa and waited. "Good morning."

The woman looked to be in her mid-thirties with fire red hair and a bright smile. She knew better than to react to the bickering between the two employees of the Katama Lodge. Elsa stepped back and greeted her warmly as Carmella beckoned for her to sit at the acupuncture table.

"I'll see you for our meeting later?" Elsa asked, her voice still fake and kind.

"Looking forward to it," Carmella affirmed as her sarcasm sizzled just beneath the surface.

When she latched the door closed, the woman on the table said, "That was some article in that Boston magazine this morning."

Carmella grimaced but forced a wider smile. "Let's just focus on what we can do for you today, huh?"

***

CARMELLA FORCED herself through her first three appointments. Toward the tail-end of the third one, Elsa texted her to come into her office for another conversation. Carmella ignored it. Instead, she headed out toward the back porch and then trailed toward the water. She felt guided there by some unknown force.

She slipped off her shoes and stood off toward the side of the beach and watched as the water traced around her toes. She had felt so big and open when she'd stood like this with Cal a few nights before. For the first time, she'd felt like more than just herself — than just Carmella.

Now, she felt even less than she had before.

The tears came shortly after that. Carmella's shoulders sagged forward as the waves continued to creep up the beach. She placed her hands over her cheeks and stared out toward the opposite island, Chappaquiddick. Always, it lurked just over in the distance — like it was another world so far away, yet close enough to see the mass of green, beauty, and beaches.

With her eyes closed, Carmella felt a presence near her. There was the soft sound of someone weeping. For a moment, Carmella thought that maybe, the weeping came from herself. But when she opened her eyes and peered toward the right end of the beach, she found none other than Helen Skarsgaard.

Helen wore a white robe, which caught the reflection of the sun beautifully. She looked angelic, like a painting in an old church, and she bent toward the water line beautifully, as though she was a part of a dance, waiting for the music to change.

Unlike Janine, Elsa, and Nancy, Carmella hadn't yet met with Helen. Now, as Helen adjusted her face and peered over toward Carmella, Carmella lifted her hand and fluttered her fingers in greeting. There they stood: two heartbroken women, at the edge of the world, looking for meaning. What did any of it mean?

Helen straightened her back. She turned her bare feet toward Carmella and walked along the edge of the sweeping water, all the way toward Carmella. Her face was blotchy and she wore no makeup. In the last film Carmella had seen of Helen, Helen had gotten into an enormous argument with the male lead — one that had made her scream and cry and throw a vase across the living room. In that, her cheeks had been streaked with black mascara. She'd told the man she would never speak to him again and then she'd fallen into a heap in the corner.

Without the makeup, Helen just looked like any other woman. She still had very beautiful features, but she could have been any other woman on the island of Martha's Vineyard, maybe en route to pick up her child at soccer practice or buy a donut at the Frosted Delights.

"Are you okay?" Helen asked softly.

Carmella shook her head. "I don't think so. And you?"

"I don't think so."

They shared a smile. For what was more intimate than shared distress? Carmella collapsed to the sand beneath them and drew her arms around her knees so that she sat like a ball. Helen joined her. Already, her robe was stained with sand and grit. The wind caught her hair beautifully, and she gazed out across the water, her eyes glistening with sorrow.

"I guess you've seen the article about the Lodge," Carmella tried after a long moment of silence.

Helen shook her head. "I didn't read it. It does me no good to read stuff like that."

Carmella nodded. She imagined that this had taken her a great deal of time to learn. It was akin to a child learning not to touch the stovetop.

"They threw me under the bus, too. And my family," Carmella

said. "This place — the Katama Lodge — it isn't always what it seems to be. I hope it's okay to tell you that."

"Nothing is ever fully what it seems to be," Helen agreed. "I've known that for years. For example, everyone thinks I'm this super successful, beautiful, happy person. And then, everyone wants to eat up the news that I'm having some kind of breakdown. They think they know the whole story! It's amazing, the things people think."

Carmella nodded. "I can't even begin to understand all of that."

Helen turned to look Carmella in the eye. "But you can. All of life is the same. We're all these scared creatures who will one day die. My husband left me, but also, what people don't know, is that I had a miscarriage and fell into such a state of depression and sorrow that I couldn't speak anymore. He had no compassion for that. And it made me realize that I was even more alone than I thought."

Carmella's throat tightened with sadness. "I am so sorry."

Helen shrugged. "I'm sure you have your own stories. Your own sorrows. Your own pain. None of it adds up to anything. It just happens to you. And then, you find a way forward. I don't know if you ever get over anything."

Carmella considered Colton, her mother, all the pain and confusion that had surrounded her father's death, and she nodded. "You're right."

"Being right doesn't fix anything, though," Helen said with an ironic laugh. "I don't know if it's better to see everything clearly or not."

"You mean, to be a little more less intelligent and a little happier?" Carmella suggested.

"Something like that," Helen said.

Carmella dropped her chin to her chest. "I am so sorry about your loss."

Helen paused for a moment. She collected her fingers together and exhaled. "Three months pregnant. I thought I'd never be happier. And then, in a flash, it was all over, taken from me. And then, my marriage was over, too. I haven't spoken to a lot of my family in years and so I came here. And I look out across the Katama Bay and I wonder what will come next."

"Just one day at a time."

"One day at a time," Helen affirmed.

CHAPTER SIXTEEN

"WHY DON'T we get out of here?" Helen turned her eyes excitedly toward Carmella's. They'd held the silence long enough and it seemed Helen had grown tired of it. She lifted from the sand, brushed the sand off her robe, and pointed for her cabin. "I just have to grab a few things."

"Where do you want to go?" In Carmella's mind, she was doomed. There was nowhere to turn.

"I don't know. Anywhere, but here. Out there, maybe." Helen nodded toward the water. "I have a sailboat on hire. We can go wherever we want. Let's sail to Europe, for crying out loud. We're free, aren't we? From everyone and everything, from expectation and from rules."

Carmella followed after her and headed toward the large cabin. Once inside, she ogled the transformation Helen had conducted within. This was no longer the cabin that she and her father had decorated a few years before. Helen had brought in a wealthy wardrobe, immaculate art, and a wide selection of sunglasses, swimsuits, large bags, and even a cat, which she stroked lovingly as she eased past the bed.

"Let's see." Helen stood before her wardrobe with her hands on her hips. "Maybe this dress?" She lifted a white lacey, strappy get-up from the right-hand side and waved it through the air. "Oh, and my yellow bikini. I always think darkness can't catch me when I wear this thing. I don't know if I'm entirely correct. And what about you? You can take whatever you want. I haven't worn half of it before. Use it like your own closet."

Carmella hesitated at the selection of swimsuits, many of which still had tags. She selected a dark red bikini, which scooped low over the breasts and lifted high on the bottoms toward the belly button. She shrugged and slipped into it in the bathroom while Helen played a selection of dance tracks from the stereo, which she'd also brought from elsewhere. When Carmella left the bathroom, Helen handed her a glass of champagne and said, "I think we should transform this day. What do you say?"

Carmella donned a black dress, a large pair of sunglasses, and a wide-brimmed hat. Helen wrapped a scarf around her head and then donned sunglasses as well. She looked the part of an old-fashioned movie star, like Marilyn Monroe on the run from the paparazzi. Carmella said this aloud, and Helen laughed. "Famous women have been on the run from the world for centuries. But the real secret is that we're actually on the run from ourselves."

Helen arranged for her driver to whisk Carmella and Helen off from the side of the parking lot. Paparazzi flung themselves after them, but the car whipped out of the parking lot and out onto the main road in such a flash that the cameramen hadn't time to grab their supplies and get into their own cars to keep up. Helen let out a laugh and dropped her head back. She looked to be the definition of freedom.

They reached the Edgartown Harbor, where a large sailboat awaited them, with a captain already on board waiting. Helen jumped on and then reached out to grab Carmella's hand to help her as she clambered aboard.

"Did you grab all the supplies I asked for?" Helen asked the man.

"I did indeed. Everything's in the fridge," the man affirmed as he reached for a rope and allowed the sails to swell with the wind.

The sailboat swept out from the docks as Helen popped the cork off of yet another bottle of champagne and poured them both sparkling glasses. They clinked them together as Helen said, "I don't know any other way to heal except to keep going."

Carmella nodded and tried out a smile. She was surprised to feel how easy it came. Maybe it was just the art of pretending that got you through. Maybe it was all in the mindset of "one day at a time," just like Helen said.

Helen removed her dress and sat in the splendor of the sun in only her bikini. Her confidence swelled across Carmella, and Carmella grabbed onto it, removing her own dress and matching Helen's pose. Compared to other summers, Carmella was a bit paler, a bit more lackluster looking and she felt a stab of sadness, as though she'd wasted too many beautiful days.

Helen removed a package of raspberries from the fridge and popped one in her mouth. As she chewed, she closed her eyes and said, "It really is the simple things, you know? I always forget that. When I was living with my husband, I swear, we spent so much money on things to try to make us happier. We bought one of those isolation tanks, and I would float in the darkness and try to pretend that I didn't have a body. And we would hire massage therapists and meditation specialists and Buddhists and — gosh, the list goes on and on. And every night as I lay there beside him, I thought about how useless it all felt. How we kept adding more things to the pile, but somehow the enormity of my feeling toward him, toward myself grew less and less."

Carmella thought about her sad little apartment, about its single chair in the kitchen — about how she'd always thought more was more, that if she had a better place, better furniture, more funds, maybe she would be happier.

"We always want what we don't have or need," she breathed.

"Yes. I had everything, and I wanted nothing."

"And I have nothing. And I want everything."

"Here's to not knowing what's right," Helen said as she lifted her glass of champagne once more.

The sailboat churned through the waves. They reached the west side of the island, where the captain dropped anchor and sat back, allowing Helen and Carmella to leap into the waves and swim around. Above them, a cliffside surged up from the water, and Carmella felt infinitely small. She rather liked that feeling as though the smaller she got, the smaller her problems were. She could hardly feel Elsa's anger anymore. She could hardly remember the face of that horrible journalist. His name? She would never speak his name again. It mattered so little to her at that moment.

"What would you have done if you hadn't been an actress?" Carmella asked Helen as they dried themselves in the sun.

Helen laughed softly. "Nobody has asked me that. Ever. Isn't that weird?"

"Kind of. Although probably, most people can't imagine that you would have wanted anything else."

"Yes. And it is true that when I was a girl, all I ever said was that I wanted to be an actress. I was in every community theater production. I was Annie and that little girl in Les Miserables and — wow, the list goes on. I haven't thought about that community theater in ages. I recently heard that they renamed the community theater after me. Helen Skarsgaard's Theater. I hate that a bit. I loved that place. I don't want it to honor me like that. I was just a small part of its history.

"But to answer your question, I don't know. I guess I really loved all my acting teachers and coaches. They just cared about acting in a pure way. They cared about storytelling. And they cared about passing along that knowledge to all of us. They were tireless in their efforts. I guess I could have seen myself doing something like that. Maybe even working at that very theater. Marrying some local guy — the football coach or a banker or whatever, and having his kids, and bringing the kids to the theater with me. Maybe we would have sat around the dinner table and acted out various performances. Maybe I would have forced everyone to do a terrible Shakespearean play. Can you imagine? All these little kids, putting on those accents. 'Tomorrow and tomorrow creeps in this petty pace from day to day...'"

Carmella laughed. "That's King Lear, isn't it?"

"Very good," Helen said.

"I don't think the world knows what a brainiac you are."

"Are you suggesting that the world thinks I'm less than?

Because I know the world thinks I'm not as smart as I am. And in some ways, I let them think that," Helen affirmed.

Carmella sipped her champagne and considered this. After a long pause, she said, "You will still have happiness. I believe you deserve it."

Helen's laugh was ironic. "I don't know. I've already gotten so many things that I wanted. Maybe I don't deserve the rest." She then peered into Carmella's eyes and said, "And what about you? What do you want?"

Carmella buzzed her lips. "I thought I wanted that guy." She'd told Helen enough about the journalist for her to understand. "But now, I don't know. I think that was just an illusion. Maybe I just want to be able to sit in the silence of myself and feel okay with myself? And maybe — well, I know I want to fix everything with my sister. And be fully honest with her for the first time about how painful it's been the past few decades."

"You owe it to yourself to be honest," Helen said. "It's the first step."

As the afternoon crept toward evening, Helen instructed the Captain to return to the Edgartown Harbor. Unfortunately, when they latched up to the creaking dock, a number of paparazzi rushed from their vehicles. It seemed like they'd been lying in wait for them. Helen's driver awaited them and attempted to block the frantic flashes of the cameras.

Midway toward the car, Carmella locked eyes with a familiar man. There, in the sea of other journalists, stood Cal himself. He dropped his camera to his chest and furrowed his brow at her, clearly aghast. Carmella's lips curled into a smile. Was this some kind of revenge that she'd spent the better part of the day with a beautiful, iconic, incredibly successful actress? It didn't feel like it to her, really, but she felt the jealousy beaming off of Cal's face.

In truth, these paparazzi just wanted whatever these beautiful creatures had. They chased them around the world for a glimpse of their wonder and fame. And Helen had simply opened her world to Carmella, without pause. She wasn't sure what it meant. Probably, it didn't mean anything.

The only important thing was that a split-second after she locked eyes with Cal, she turned her gaze toward the car and marched past him as though she'd never met him in her life.

Once in the back of the car, Helen let out another whoop. "Thank goodness for these tinted windows," she said of the car. "Idiots."

"That journalist was there," Carmella said softly.

Helen's eyebrows rose. "You're kidding."

"No."

"He's a scavenger, Carmella. Gosh, it makes me so mad that he ever used you like that. As someone who has been used time and time again, I know it's one of the worst things to feel," Helen admitted, placing a tender hand on her arm.

Carmella watched Cal out of the window as the car ducked back onto the road and rushed them back to the Katama Lodge. He looked confused and at a loss. She couldn't contain her grin and she was grateful for that. Maybe, in some small way, she would stick in his mind as a woman he couldn't fully trap with his words.

CHAPTER SEVENTEEN

WHEN CARMELLA RETURNED to the Lodge, she walked past Elsa's office. There was murmuring through the door — Janine's voice, then Nancy's, then Elsa's. Probably, they were trying to decide what to do to get out in front of this PR disaster. As Carmella paused there, Jennifer Conrad bustled in through the front door, gave Carmella an anxious smile, and then knocked at the door. She'd been called in to rectify any bad social media that had been circulating. What could they possibly post to void the article? How could they get back on track?

Carmella checked her appointment schedule. She had one final client in thirty minutes and then she was home free. What would she do with the strange evening ahead? She immediately texted Cody.

CARMELLA: Can I steal you tonight?

CODY: I'm guessing you need mental health assistance?

CARMELLA: Don't remind me.

CODY: I won't. We don't have to talk about it at all. I'll buy wine. And provisions.

CARMELLA: What kind of provisions?

CODY: The Ben and Jerry's kind.

Carmella forced herself through her final appointment of the day, then headed back into the hallway. Elsa's door was opened just a crack. Carmella stuck her foot into it and opened it even more. Elsa sat at the edge of her desk and stared out the window. She didn't turn to face Carmella, but she knew it was her.

"I don't know if I feel up for talking to you right now," Elsa said.

Carmella's heart felt cracked. "There are so many things I need to say."

Elsa drew her hands over her eyes and heaved a sigh. "Maybe. Maybe soon. But not today, Carmella. There's already been too much. To read about all of this? Online? Our family story plastered across headlines like this? I just don't know what to make of it." A sob escaped her throat.

Carmella dropped her eyes to the ground. She considered again what her therapist had said. "You deserve to tell your story, just as much as Elsa deserves to hear it." But she knew a closed door when she saw one. She stepped back into the foyer and headed for her car. Closure was maybe a thing other people got. Not her.

She arrived at Cody's house fifteen minutes later. When she reached his door, she heard his panicked voice inside. "What did you say? Fiona, stop crying! I can't understand what happened. I can't—"

Carmella tried the door and found it open. She pushed it open to discover Cody at his kitchen table, bent over his chair. His cheeks were streaked with red.

"She fell? Off her tricycle?"

Silence again. Carmella's heart dropped into her gut. What was it about today? Was the entire world off-kilter?

Cody lifted his chin and beckoned for Carmella to come in. She shifted forward, then closed the door behind her. Cody splayed a hand over his forehead and nodded as he continued to speak into the phone.

"I don't think that's bad enough for a hospital run, Fi. It sounds like she just got scared and started crying."

Carmella sat at the edge of his couch and pressed her palms together. She hated when he called his ex "Fi." She wasn't sure why. It added this familiarity that Carmella didn't fully like. But who was she to think like that? They'd been married; they had a child together. She couldn't comprehend that level of familiarity.

"Maybe an ice pack? It'll stop the swelling," Cody suggested then. After another pause, he said, "I don't think it's necessary for me to come over, Fi. I've had her the past few nights and I told Carmella that I—"

Again, silence as Fiona spoke on the other end. Carmella felt suddenly deep underwater.

"Don't say that," Cody offered softly. "That's so cruel, Fiona."

Cruel? What had she said? Carmella furrowed her brow and stared at the far corner, praying for this awkward moment to die out.

"Fiona, I just don't think it's a good idea," Cody said then. "Really. You know when we spend more time together, we just fight."

More silence.

"Yes, I do think it would be like that this time. Yes, I know you've been going to therapy. I've been going, too. I just still don't think our problems are resolved enough to give it—"

Again, silence.

"I understand. And yes, I'll think about it. Yes, I promise I will. Okay. Kiss Gretchen for me. Tell her I love her. Tell her to get well soon."

Cody hung up the phone and pressed it against his chest. It took him a long time to face Carmella. When he did, his eyes seemed very far away.

"What happened?" Carmella asked.

"Just a little accident. Typical of toddlers," Cody said. "But Fiona is dramatic. And she's overwhelmed. And she wants me to come over."

"Do you want to?"

Cody shrugged. "I never really know. Sometimes, she asks if I want to try again."

"Try again?"

"To be together. To have a family with Gretchen."

Carmella's heart dropped even lower.

"But I force myself to remember how bad it was to be together. It was awful. We fought all the time. It was such a poisonous environment to have a baby in. But reminding her of that just hurts her. She asks if she's not good enough for me and it's all so pointed and jarring and it really breaks me up inside. And then, stuff like this happens, and she's like, 'Why can't we just live together as a family?' and it just kills me."

Carmella suddenly felt as though her problems were terribly small.

"Do you think you still love her?" she asked softly.

"It doesn't really matter. I see it all out in front of me — the big mess of it all and I know that we can't go back that," Cody said. "No matter how much I wish we could, sometimes."

"Do you really wish that?"

"I don't know. Maybe."

Carmella felt even sourer than she had before. Why was that? Cody stood and headed for the fridge, where he removed a bottle of wine. He cracked it open and then poured them both half-filled glasses.

"I hope I'm not making a mistake," he said, mostly to himself.

"In what, exactly?"

"In not going over there. In not being there for Gretchen. In not getting back together with Fiona. I don't know. Being an adult just means being wracked with guilt all the time."

"I definitely feel all that guilt and more today," Carmella said. "And a hangover the size of Texas."

"Right." Cody arched an eyebrow. "Do you want to talk about him at all?"

"Only the ways we'll murder him in cold blood," Carmella said. She then buzzed her lips and said, "I'm just grateful that I didn't go all the way with him."

Cody's shoulders slumped forward the slightest bit. "I wondered about that. You didn't check your phone till the morning."

"Yeah. I fell asleep at the Sunrise Cove. I had to do some kind of weird walk of shame through the foyer of the inn. Although I don't know if it's a walk of shame, officially, if I didn't actually do the deed?"

"I don't know. We'll have to check the definition," Cody said playfully.

Maybe they could find a way through this dark time together.

They drank their first glass of wine. Cody confessed he was starving, that he'd skipped lunch that afternoon, and they decided to head to the diner for an official "sad person dinner."

"It didn't use to be sad to go to the diner," Carmella said as she stepped into the heat of the evening.

"Grilled cheese sandwiches and burgers really do transition from being everyday fare to, 'Oh my God, I'm dying. I need comfort food,'" Cody admitted. "What's that about?"

"We reach for nostalgia at every turn," Carmella said.

"Something like that."

CHAPTER EIGHTEEN

CARMELLA AND CODY walked the route to the diner. Cody was despondent. His eyes scanned the waters as they creaked along the boardwalk, and his hand twitched toward his pocket as though he remembered something urgent he needed to do and then pushed the thought away. Carmella remembered all the other times he'd been similar to this — times Cody's eyes had seemed lackluster and faraway, times she'd drummed through her wide treasure-trove of memories of their time together in order to cheer him up. She reached up and gripped his elbow and squeezed just once, a thing she had done when they'd been teenagers, but he hardly smiled at all. He was like a ghost. Maybe they all were.

The waitress they knew well, the eighteen-year-old whip-smart yet growing more pregnant by the day, Mandy, Amelia Taylor's niece — drew open the door with the jangle of the bell and greeted them warmly. As she did, she spoke off to the side to one of the fry cooks, saying, "Yeah, Chelsea and Xav already have a pretty good set-up, I guess. I'll head to Brooklyn to see them before the baby comes.

Chelsea had worked at the diner for years but had recently headed off to Brooklyn to make something of herself, along with her boyfriend, that dark and brooding teen, Xavier. Again, Carmella marveled at the bravery of such young people, off to craft a world of their own design without a worry in the world. To be young and untouchable.

"Hi, there!" Mandy said brightly. "We aren't so busy tonight, so grab a booth wherever you please. That one over by the jukebox has your name on it, as usual, I guess. Can I grab you some milkshakes to get you started?"

Her energy buzzed wildly. Carmella hesitated, glanced toward Cody, and then forced herself to nod. "That would be great."

"Just coffee for me," Cody interjected.

Carmella's smile faltered a bit. "Okay. Maybe no milkshakes today, then."

"Two coffees?"

"Sure."

Carmella led Cody off to their traditional booth. Mandy lay two sticky menus onto the table and then sauntered off to pour them two mugs of coffee. Cody placed his face in his hands for a long, uncomfortable moment. Carmella's heart beat like a drum at war — monstrously loud and ominous. Her mind continued to flash with images from the previous twenty-four hours. She felt she staggered through the remainder of it; the path toward midnight was made of jagged rock.

"You want a burger?" she finally asked Cody.

Cody grumbled. "I guess."

"And we can share fries and onion rings?"

"Sure."

Carmella gave the order to Mandy when she returned with their coffees. Cody stared into the glistening dark liquid. Her heart aching, Carmella reached for her purse and drew out three dollar bills, enough money for six songs on the jukebox. Hurriedly, she rushed for the old machine, as though it and it alone could bring healing and peace to their strange day. Within the next minute, she'd selected Fugee's "Killing Me Softly," which she and Cody traditionally sang at the top of their lungs for all to hear.

Back at the table, Cody ripped open his sugar packets and dropped the morsels into the liquid. He stirred with a small spoon; it clacked against the sides of the mug.

"Remember this, Code?" Carmella tried. "I particularly remember that night after prom when we drove around and belted this out as loud as we could."

Cody nodded the slightest bit as though this was a memory far beneath the surface for him — nothing he could fully draw up any longer. "Yeah. Fun, wild times."

Carmella swallowed the lump in her throat. She sipped her coffee which was absolutely terrible, probably something they'd brewed up about seven hours before when normal people drank coffee. She wanted a milkshake; she wanted her best friend to act like her best friend; she wanted to take back every silly thing she'd done over the previous twenty-four hours and sleep like an innocent child again. It was too much to ask.

When Fugees finished, up came Fleetwood Mac's "*Everywhere*," another of their favorites. Cody's eyes brightened just the slightest bit.

"Guess you played all of our tunes, huh?"

"Only the best for you," Carmella affirmed.

Cody's phone buzzed. He dotted a finger on it and drew up a number of messages, all from Fiona. He grumbled inwardly.

"What did she say?"

"I don't know. It doesn't matter."

"It matters to me."

Cody arched an eyebrow. He looked on the verge of disputing this fact. Carmella rose up and told him she planned to go to the bathroom. She walked in time to Fleetwood Mac, all the way to the stall, where she collapsed on the toilet seat and placed her face in her hands. Once there, she too received a message.

CAL: I couldn't believe you stepped off that boat with Helen Skarsgaard.

CAL: I should have known better than to comprehend what kind of woman you were.

CAL: You can't be caged ;)

Carmella's throat closed at the thought of him actually scribing these words. What purpose did he think they had? She knew he only wanted to get close to her again to hear more about what had happened with Helen, about her innermost secrets. Carmella couldn't believe she had allowed some quasi-handsome reporter to make her so weak at the knees that she'd given him so much of her soul. The soul was a funny thing once you revealed it to others, you couldn't necessarily get it back.

CARMELLA: Never contact me again.

She then immediately blocked him. This was at least a bit empowering. It was up to her to draw a line in the sand around her own emotions. Men like Cal weren't allowed in. Never again, that is.

Again, she thanked her lucky stars that all she'd done was kiss him. She hadn't given him everything. And now, she would spend the rest of her life forgetting his name.

When Carmella returned to the dining area, the jukebox switched over to the classic '90s hit, "Nothing Compares 2 U" by Sinead O'Connor. For years, she and Cody had imitated the music video — attempting to make themselves cry, like Sinead, and staring at one another bug-eyed until one or the other started to laugh instead.

"It's been seven hours and fifteen days..." Carmella began as she slid into the booth.

Cody was curled strangely over the table. Again, he had his hands over his cheeks. His forehead was wrinkled as though he was deep in thought. He didn't play along. In fact, he looked on the verge of some kind of breakdown.

Mandy arrived with their platters of food. She arched an eyebrow at Cody, made eye contact with Carmella, then walked off to attend to another table.

"Code? Can you at least tell me what's up?"

Carmella reached for a French fry and ripped it in half. She then placed the piping hot potato on her tongue and waited. Finally, Cody lifted his face to show red-rimmed eyes.

"You did it," Carmella said.

Cody furrowed his brow even more. "Did what?"

"You cried during 'Nothing Compares 2 U.' Just like we always tried to make ourselves do."

"Oh. Yep. I guess I did." His voice was heavy with sarcasm.

Carmella's heart darkened. "Did Fiona text you again?"

"Not exactly."

The conversation was strained. Carmella chewed at her lower lip and then ate another fry. She and Cody had had off days before for sure, but this was something else. She felt outside her element, uncomfortable.

"Carmella, these songs just bring up complicated memories for me, okay?"

Carmella's jaw dropped. "What do you mean?"

"I just mean, Carm — they're beautiful memories, but they're ours. They belong to the two of us. And it just reminds me how much I — gosh, forget it. You don't want to hear it. Not after the day you've had."

Carmella was flustered. She wrapped a strand of hair behind her ear and gaped at him. "Cody, please. If I've made you upset, I want to know why."

Cody's nostrils flared. "Year after year, I was there for you. You were my everything, Carmella. You were always in so much pain, and I knew that, and I always waited for you and wanted you to be comfortable and happy. And I told myself, maybe we'll figure it out sooner than later. Maybe we'll find a way to be together then. But year after year, you just grew darker and angrier. And you seemed like you wanted nothing to do with me. And now, we're here. We're middle-aged, dammit. At least, right now, I feel pretty stinkin' old. And our lives have passed us by. I don't want to be reminded of all the times we could have been together. I don't want to be reminded of the greatest loss of my life. And I know how selfish that sounds. Look, I have you here. You're my best friend. I guess that should be enough."

Cody lifted the mug of coffee and drank down the rest. He then glanced at his food, grimaced and shot up from the booth. Carmella gaped at him. He seemed unwilling to allow her to speak. He paused just over the table as the last beats of "*Nothing Compares 2 U*" came through the old speakers.

"I've been there for you on every bad day, in every way that I could be," he said finally. "And I don't know if you were just too selfish to notice my love for you, or you just didn't want to, but here we are. Forty-two years old. And I have a child to care for and a potential ex-wife to get back together with. I don't know. Maybe it's time we take a break. Maybe that's the healthy thing to do."

Carmella reached out and gripped Cody's wrist. His eyes found hers for the shortest, briefest, most powerful of seconds. He then drew his hand away and marched for the door. Carmella sat in dismay as her thoughts raced through her mind. Another song played on the jukebox, The Kinks' "*This Time Tomorrow*," which now was the equivalent of feeling a punch to the stomach. Carmella's eyes stung with tears.

It had been a perfectly horrible day — the kind of days Shakespeare wrote three-hour plays about. Carmella drew her neck forward and let out a long, slow sob. Mandy rushed for her table with a milkshake.

"Thank you. That is so sweet." Carmella gasped as terror wrapped around her heart. Tears drew long streaks down her cheeks. She had literally no idea how to go through life without Cody. He was her rock. He was her map. He was her everything.

"You like strawberries, don't you?"

Carmella lifted her eyes to Mandy's. She tried to understand the question. "What?"

"I mean the milkshake. It's the kind I made you. I was pretty sure you liked this flavor."

"Oh, gosh. Yes. I do." Carmella stabbed a straw into the center of the icy delight and sucked slowly. The sugar felt like a crime. What the hell was she doing there all alone at the diner she so loved, without the best friend she loved the most?

"Please, let me know if I can do anything," Mandy told her. There was none of that funny teenager sarcasm to her words. Maybe, already, she'd begun to reckon with the fact that life was a sad and dark thing, sometimes. Maybe, already, she'd begun to soften her edges.

"There's nothing to be done. I already made all the mistakes a long time ago," Carmella offered with a dry laugh. "I guess now I have to stare them straight in the face."

CHAPTER NINETEEN

CARMELLA WASN'T FULLY sure how to get through the night. Her heart raced her toward very near panic attacks and her thoughts purred loud into a violent roar that had her pressing her hands to her ears, an attempt to make them stop. She paced back and forth in her apartment, sipping wine late into the night. She had brought French fries and onion rings back from the diner, her only sustenance for most of the day, and she barreled toward midnight, then two and then four.

She'd only texted Cody once in the wake of his storming out.

CARMELLA: Please. Just talk to me. Let's talk about this the way we've talked about everything else. I want to be there for you in everything.

There was so much to say aloud. It suddenly seemed as though the events with that stupid journalist, Cal, meant absolutely nothing. Carmella now felt all the words from Elsa, Karen, Nancy, and even her father over the years. "That Cody would do anything for you." Then, the knowing looks. Carmella had always slightly resented that any relationship between a boy and a girl was always reduced to "are they romantically involved?" Cody meant the world to her. Their relationship had nothing to do with other relationships she'd heard of over the years — the ones that had resulted in boxes of belongings thrown out of windows, tense fights about things like which coffee tables to buy and where to put them in the house and who would get the coffee tables during the inevitable divorce, things that made Carmella's head spin around with sorrow. Those silly, romantic-turned-dark relationships had nothing to do with her and Cody.

But now, now he'd made his big confession. And with this confession, he'd attributed something to her that she didn't fully like. She had been selfish. All these years, she had considered only her heartache, her sorrow — the fact that it had been her fault and only her fault, all the events that had gone wrong. There had been so many other people in the picture. She hadn't been alone; she had just told herself a story of loneliness that she'd believed in, a story that had grown almost impenetrable over the years. Yet here and now, it had begun to crumble.

Around five in the morning, Carmella made peace with the fact that she wouldn't sleep. She stepped into the shower and scrubbed herself clean, digging her nails deep into her skull in an attempt to wake herself up still more. By six, her hair was dry, and she adjusted herself into a dark burgundy dress with a turtle neckline. The reflection in the mirror told a story of a beautiful, middle-aged woman who was brave enough to face all the trauma, all the pain, the immensity of the story of her life, and make something of it. At least, she had to believe that.

Carmella sat out in the sun on the back porch of the Katama Lodge. Nancy stepped out from her first yoga class of the day. She wore a tight-fitting tank-top and a pair of stretchy pants, and her hair was scooped up into a vibrant ponytail. Sometimes, it was difficult to remember that this woman was fifty-nine years old.

Her eyes didn't smile when she spotted Carmella. Her lips curved up the slightest bit — maybe a nervous tick. Carmella rose from the rocking chair and lifted a hand.

"Could we talk for a moment, Nancy?"

Nancy paused for the slightest moment. Her shoulders curved forward. "Elsa and I still haven't come to any kind of conclusion about what to do."

"I understand," Carmella breathed.

"Elsa is devastated. You know what this place means to her. And it means all that to me, too. We thought it meant something to you."

Carmella's throat tightened. "It always has. It means everything to me."

Nancy gave a half-hearted shrug. "I don't know what to say. I just, I—" She paused for a long time and wiped a patch of sweat from her forehead. "I have to meet Helen down at her cabin for a private session. But maybe we can talk more about this later."

"I hope so," Carmella replied.

Nancy heaved a sigh. "Remember what I said to you and Elsa last month? About learning to bridge beyond your differences? About learning to love one another properly?"

Carmella remembered it well. It was a crazy, screaming version of Nancy in the kitchen, a woman who demanded she and Elsa take a second look at the destructive relationship they'd built for themselves over the years.

"I really thought we were close to building something again," Carmella said as her voice cracked.

"Maybe there's still hope," Nancy offered. "I just don't know."

———

LATER THAT EVENING, Carmella found herself at The Hesson House's outdoor dining area, where Lola Sheridan had agreed to meet her. Lola sat with a glass of chardonnay at one of the far-off tables, closer to the dock. The last of the evening light seemed to burrow itself within that single glass of wine — almost as though it had magical properties. Lola glanced up and delivered a vibrant smile, then beckoned for Carmella to sit. Carmella's heart skipped a beat all over again. When she had called Lola earlier that afternoon with her proposition, she hadn't thought for a moment Lola would go for it.

"Hey! I just got off the phone with my editor," Lola started as Carmella slid into the chair across from her. "I thought I wouldn't get through to him today. He took the week off to build sandcastles on the beach with his kids, apparently — and he says he's miserable. He misses the newsroom. Isn't that ridiculous?"

Carmella wasn't exactly in the mood for this kind of light banter, but she heard herself laugh, then felt herself toss her head back, as though this was the most fascinating story in the world.

"At any rate, I told him about the article, which he'd already read, and also about the counter article that you and I have already discussed. The only thing is for him to agree to it — we really need that interview with Helen."

Carmella pressed her lips together. This was the tricky part. It added a level of power to their article that Cal's had lacked, which was the "straight from the horse's mouth" element, that would come from Helen herself. Carmella had seen Helen only once that day, during which she'd been in close conversation with Janine as tears had glittered around her eyes. It hadn't been a particularly good time to bring up something like an interview.

"Do you think she'll go for it?"

"I really have no idea," Carmella said finally. She felt strange and despondent and outside of herself. "But if it's my only chance, then I guess I have to ask her."

"Do. And tell her it's for the Lodge, you know? The Katama Lodge has gone all out for her over the past week. Your lives have been affected. And now, in the wake of that article, it's frankly possible that your revenue will slant downward."

"We've already received several requests for cancellations for the next few months," Carmella affirmed softly.

"Shoot. People love to read slander, don't they? It's the one thing that sells. And as a journalist, I remember being twenty-one, twenty-two, with a very young daughter to feed and contemplating if I would drop down low enough to write anything, like tabloid trash, that would put a paycheck in my hand and food on my table."

"Did you?"

"No. I didn't. But I sometimes wonder how much easier my life would have been if I'd just done some sort of article about Kate Winslet's bra size or Colin Firth's love life."

Carmella chuckled appreciatively. "But you've managed it without all the filth and ruining someone's life."

"I have. Somehow, it all worked out. Sometimes, I have to pinch myself when I remember the past," Lola said. Her eyes grew suddenly shadowed and far away. "Oh, but this isn't about me. Talk to Helen. I'll get cracking on what you've already given me. And you said something about Henry's documentary?"

"Yes," Carmella affirmed. "Janine's boyfriend. He filmed loads of interviews with women who've spent time at the Lodge over the years. I think it was mostly through the lens of what the Lodge and Neal meant to these people because Janine wanted to show it to Nancy, her mother, as some sort of — hmm. How do I put it?"

"Like, she wanted to show Nancy that she appreciated how much she'd done here on the Vineyard?"

"Something like that." Carmella paused and turned her gaze toward the water. "I've always felt that other people are much better at resolving their conflicts and moving forward than I am. It's like I always cling to my grudges like my life depends upon them."

Lola frowned the slightest bit. She seemed to take Carmella's words and roll them about, give them their full weight. "I'm sure you will find a way to let go of them when you're ready. Maybe you're just not ready yet."

Carmella's smile grew wider as the inner aching of her soul grew heavier. "Maybe. Or maybe I'll just be terribly frightened forever. And I'll die knowing that I didn't take every risk."

Lola splayed her hand over Carmella's and held her gaze. "If you can already see the potential for this, then maybe you can fight it. It doesn't have to be your destiny if you don't want it to be. All I can say is this. Until last year, my sisters and I refused to speak with one another. Our father was our greatest enemy. And now, we all live here, on this gorgeous island, together. It's never too late to be or do anything you want to do. Make every decision with love and forgiveness, especially with forgiveness and tenderness toward yourself."

That night, Carmella drove back to the Katama Lodge. She told the head guard that she needed to grab something in her office, swept down the hallway, then weaved her way to the front desk, where she was able to dial Helen's cabin all the way down by the water. It was better to call. A knock at the door was ominous and invasive. This way, Helen always had the option not to answer.

Helen's dreamy, soothing voice answered on the third ring. When she discovered who it was, she immediately invited Carmella down to her cabin. Carmella had the frantic energy of a much younger girl. She whisked down the hill between the greater Lodge and her cabin, then appeared at the door as Helen swung it open. She looked every bit the part of a "movie star" on the verge of retiring for the night. She wore an enormous, fluffy robe, one that swept out in a more cape-like fashion than ones Carmella remembered her mother wearing back in the old days. Her hair was bulbous and it cascaded down her shoulders marvelously, and she smiled as though she'd had one too many glasses of wine in preparation of embarking to dreamland.

"Carmella, I'm so glad to see you," she said as she beckoned for Carmella to enter. She poured her a glass of champagne and watched with cat-like eyes as Carmella collapsed on the yellow couch. She was perched beside a large potted plant, one that, it seemed, Helen had shipped in even since Carmella's sailing expedition with her.

"I suppose you're still reeling after everything that happened?"

Carmella puffed out her cheeks. "It seems like everything always happens at once. And now, my best friend has turned on me."

Helen arched an eyebrow. "You're feeling lonely."

"That's an understatement."

"Welcome to the club. You've come to the right place." Helen's laughter was like music. "But you knew that."

"I guess I knew that."

Helen lifted her glass of champagne and clinked it against Carmella's. They shared a moment of silence before they sipped. Carmella imagined that each of the popping champagne bubbles upon her tongue cost upwards of two hundred dollars.

"How are you feeling?" Carmella asked.

"That's a very good question. I wish I knew the answer."

Carmella nodded.

"Your sisters and stepmother have been so generous toward me," Helen continued. "They're the type of women who've seen tremendous pain and understand a little bit better how to handle mine own. I feel I don't go to them and just drop all my pain at the door. Instead, they help me find ways to cope and heal. Janine said something about feeling everything, accepting the wholeness of it, and then moving forward."

"Don't judge yourself for your feelings, I suppose. Such a tricky task," Carmella said.

"Tricky indeed. Of course, I'm sure your sisters and stepmother told you how difficult I was to manage during my first days here. So resistant, if only because I stirred in such self-hatred."

"They understood."

Carmella licked her lips, sipped her champagne a final time, and then said, "That article really damaged the Lodge. It's all my fault. I don't know how I can ever find a way back to my sisters or my stepmother. I honestly don't know how they could ever forgive me."

"The press is a horrific thing— only out for sales and not caring who they destroy in the process."

"But don't you think sometimes, it could do beautiful things? If given the right material."

Helen bowed her head the slightest bit. Realization seemed to pass over her.

"I don't mean to be invasive. I don't want you to do anything you don't want to do," Carmella said then, as softly as she could.

"No. No. It makes sense. It does. It's partially my fault that this article was written to begin with." Helen sipped another bit of champagne and nodded. "I won't talk about anything that happened in my life."

"You wouldn't have to. Only about the Lodge and your experience."

"Just about the Lodge," Helen agreed. "And what a remarkable place it is. Your sisters keep telling me that I can leave whenever I want. My only question to them is, where else on this earth would I possibly want to go?"

CHAPTER TWENTY

IT WAS the last Saturday in August. Carmella stood on the tiny, made-for-one porch that hung off of her apartment building and sipped her steaming coffee with her chin lifted toward the sky. In some respects, the August sun steamed hotter than ever, but occasionally, when the breeze sliced just right, she felt it: that sinister creak toward autumn. She wondered what the next months would hold. Perhaps she would be just as lonely as the previous years or perhaps even worse, as she no longer had Cody by her side, either.

Cody had finally texted her, but only to tell her that he still needed to think, to decompress. He had a lot on his mind and he wasn't sure he could trust himself to say the right thing. Carmella's response had been: "You're my best friend. I never need you to say the right thing. I only want you to say what's in your heart." But he hadn't responded. Perhaps it had been too heavy, what she'd said. Perhaps she would never fully know.

When she asked her own heart what she felt about Cody, about the love between them, she faltered slightly. It was so difficult to comprehend what that would mean. They had hardly ever held hands. In therapy, Carmella had brought up the concept, and her therapist had dug into the idea of "intimacy" problems, about whether or not Carmella could really let people beyond her personal-built boundaries. Carmella had chuckled at the thought. "Let people in through these immensely thick walls, which I've spent the previous thirty years building? I won't fall the way Rome did. I'm not stupid."

Her therapist had laughed at her joke, but she'd also scribbled something in her notepad, which had left Carmella tossing and turning throughout the night. What had she written? Probably something like, "Uses humor to deflect." That was true, wasn't it? Not a whole lot to unpack there.

"What is your ideal life, a year from now?" her therapist had asked her recently. "Picture it. Tell me what it's like. Where are you? Are you on the Vineyard? Are you far away?"

Carmella had closed her eyes and really, really tried to envision the next steps of the course of her life. Unfortunately, she had seen only the grey shimmer of light behind her eyelids. She laughed again and told her therapist that she'd always thought she was more creative than all this. "I guess not." It hadn't been the most productive of therapy sessions.

Carmella wandered back inside, washed her coffee mug, dried it, and then placed it back on its shelf, alongside her other three. She so rarely had anyone over for coffee. She so rarely had anyone over at all.

Her phone buzzed. The name on the message was Elsa's.

Carmella hadn't heard from her at all in days. She drew open the message and read it once, twice, then again, as her heart fluttered with excitement.

ELSA: Hey, Carm. We're having a BBQ at the house. We'd love for you to join.

It was a second olive branch. Carmella hadn't imagined a world in which she'd been allowed that. She quickly wrote back a resounding yes, then lay back on her bed and practiced, over and over again, the appropriate words to say to the sister she loved so much. "I'm sorry. I just really liked him and I lost my head. I'm sorry. You and the Katama Lodge mean more to me than I can possibly express. I'm sorry. How many ways can I say the words, I'm sorry?" She sounded frantic. She was reminded of long-ago days when she'd been so excited that Elsa had invited her for silly things with her much older friends — like watching a PG-13 movie or staying up till midnight playing on the internet. Little slivers of Elsa's life, which Elsa had had total control over but could give to Carmella or deny.

This felt like a gift.

Carmella went to the local natural wine store and selected a bottle. While she waited for the cashier, she noted the pile of newspapers off to the side of the register. They all held today's news — wars, gossip columns, oil shortages, everyday horrors and everyday triumphs. The article about Katama Lodge was now in the past. You couldn't purchase it anywhere any longer. This had to be some sort of a triumph. They were headed toward the future.

Mallory stood out in front of the house with Zachery across her chest. She spoke on the phone with Lucas; at least that's what Carmella assumed based on the tough tone she administered.

"I can't take him tomorrow. You know that I have to work at the Lodge," Mallory said as she gave Carmella a distracted smile. "And I know you only want to get out to see your friends."

Carmella swept past Mallory, praying that this Lucas guy would get his act together. If he didn't, she prayed that Mallory would find a way past him. She prayed the heartache wouldn't cut too deep.

Carmella appeared at the edge of the screen door, which separated the house with the large porch that extended out toward the beach. She inhaled slowly and then reached for the door handle. Just before she unlatched it, however, she heard her name and paused on instinct. Perhaps she shouldn't have. Perhaps she should have burst in, despite everything, and pushed beyond this torment.

"It's absolute defamation," Bruce said, his voice deep and brooding. "I wouldn't totally rule out suing this guy. He took advantage of Carmella."

"I know, but I mean, she walked right into his trap, didn't she?" Elsa returned.

Sweat billowed on the back of Carmella's neck. Now she knew, fully, that her sister thought she was some selfish idiot. Great.

"Come on, Elsa. These guys can be master manipulators," Bruce returned in Carmella's defense. "I've worked with enough characters like this to know how they operate. It's not pretty. They'll do everything to get their piece which would include selling their newborn."

"I'm just not fully sure she didn't partially do it on purpose," Elsa returned.

Carmella's heart sunk to the pit of her stomach. This was the worst slap in the face.

"Why do you say that?"

"Well, I mean, I've talked to you a bit about our family history. It has a lot of complexities."

"Yes. A bit."

"I just always know that Carmella blamed herself— for Colton. And she always thought our parents blamed her for it, too. She took the blame and carried it on her shoulders for all these years. And sometimes, she woke up in the middle of the night screaming and crying and I would go in and try to comfort her and put her back to sleep. But it destroyed me to see her like that."

"Was she asleep?"

"She was still dreaming, yes," Elsa replied.

"Did you ever tell her that you found her like this?"

Elsa was silent. Carmella's eyes now welled with tears.

"I wish I could tell you that my mother and father didn't treat her differently," Elsa said then, her own voice breaking. "But I don't know. I can't remember. It's a true thing that sometimes, parents treat their children differently — they play favorites. Did that happen to us? I don't know. We were all so young and then Colton was gone and there was so much trauma. Nobody ever dealt with it the right way. The way I dealt with it was to fall in love with Aiden and start building a family. Carmella aligned herself with Karen, and then bam, Karen was gone. She resented Dad in a lot of ways. They just never saw eye-to-eye."

"And now, he's gone," Bruce finished.

There was silence at the table. Finally, Elsa said, "I just wish Carmella would have told me some of these things herself."

"Why did you invite her today?"

"I spoke with Helen Skarsgaard last night. She'd just done an interview with Lola Sheridan about the Katama Lodge. She explained that Carmella arranged it in a kind of push-back against the awful article that Cal had written."

"Carmella arranged it?"

"Apparently, and the way Helen spoke about Carmella was like she knew a version of Carmella that I've never met. I would like to meet that version, but I don't know how or if she's willing to open up to me like that. I don't know how to break down her barriers. I know we started a few weeks ago, but it all felt like it was false and forced. Gosh, Bruce, I'm telling you too much, aren't I? In a relative sense, I've just met you."

"Don't worry yourself," Bruce returned.

Carmella stepped back from the screen door. Her tears had now fully streaked her cheeks. She wasn't sure how to enter this scene. She felt like a deleted character in a film, as though her scene had been scrapped because the movie was too long and complicated already. She just stood there not knowing what to do, then she continued to hover, until all too soon, Elsa appeared in the screen door and bucked back, surprised.

"Carmella!" Her eyes connected with hers through the screen. She gave no smile. "Carmella," she echoed. "How long have you been standing there?"

Carmella wiped her cheeks clean of tears. She then lifted the natural bottle of wine and said, "It doesn't matter."

Elsa opened the door so that the screen door screeched like a wild animal. Their eyes fully connected, now.

"I just never got over it," Carmella finally said. These were words she'd never said to anyone, yet they sizzled with the truth. "I never got over Colton's death. He was my best friend, Elsa. And then, I made one wrong move, and he was gone forever. I just couldn't fathom that. It made me feel as though every other decision I made for the rest of my life would result in something similarly awful. I grew totally paralyzed over the years. I haven't been able to fall in love or have babies or make anything out of my life, all because of that day. And I know it killed pieces of Mom and Dad, too."

Elsa's own eyes now welled with tears. "They didn't blame you, Carm. They couldn't have. You were just a kid. It was an accident."

"I know. But I just worried — heck, I still worry that they built up some kind of irrational hatred toward me."

Elsa shook her head. She then stepped through the doorway and flung her arms around Carmella. She shook violently with sorrow as Carmella dug her chin into Elsa's shoulder.

"They didn't hate you. They loved you so much!" Elsa cried. "And I love you, more than words, more than life itself. Carmella, don't you know how much I love you?" She leaned back and gripped Carmella's shoulders. Her eyes were formidable and violent in their blue coloring.

At that moment, Nancy, Janine, Mallory, and baby Zachery entered the house on the other side of the living area. Carmella flung her head around to catch sight of them — a beautiful mixed family of strong women.

"Well, Carmella! I didn't know you were coming for the barbecue!" Nancy cried. There wasn't a single air of anger behind her words.

Janine rushed across the room and joined the two girls in a

group hug. "I spoke with Helen just now! She said she talked endless poetics about our Katama Lodge to Lola Sheridan for that article. I think we're going to be okay. We're really going to be okay."

The hug was one of endless warmth. It reminded Carmella of being a little girl, all wrapped up in the arms of her mother post-bath. She remembered that her mother used to put her towel in the dryer for a few minutes before bath time to allow her to enclose Carmella in the most tender of embraces.

They sat out on the porch, just as they had done a thousand times before, as Bruce cranked up the grill. Henry arrived shortly after. He greeted everyone and then dotted a kiss directly on Janine's lips — a fact that made her cheeks burn crimson. A few minutes later, Alyssa, Janine's youngest, arrived with a wide selection of fruits, vegetables, and bags of chips. "I couldn't decide on whether or not I wanted to be healthy or not," she admitted with a shrug. "So I thought it was better to have options."

"Oh, Carm. You should really invite Cody tonight!" Elsa said brightly as she rose up to help Bruce with something at the grill.

Carmella's heart banged away with sorrow. "I don't know. He said he's busy with something tonight."

"Oh, shoot. Something with Gretchen?"

"Yeah. You know how it is."

"He must be one of the best dads ever," Elsa affirmed. "He's so kind and considerate. I can't believe Fiona bailed on him. She should have clung to that guy with everything she had."

Carmella's eyes threatened to spill tears again. Thankfully, Elsa turned back to the grill and splayed each chicken breast with homemade BBQ sauce. Nancy began to talk excitedly to Janine about a new yoga technique she had recently refined, while Alyssa and Mallory flipped through a magazine with "best summer styles" splayed on every page. Carmella wanted to remind the girls that summer was very nearly over; these were the final days of it. But why would she bring such darkness to such a glorious day? The old Carmella would have done that. Not her. Not now.

CHAPTER TWENTY-ONE

"THERAPY?" Elsa stood in the doorway of Carmella's acupuncturist room and crossed her arms over her chest. "You've been going? All this time?"

"Not a really long time," Carmella admitted. She adjusted a gold earring into her right ear and forced herself to look Elsa in the eye. "But she did say it would benefit us to maybe go together. If you'd be game for that."

Elsa dropped her gaze to the floor. It was clear that for Elsa, the idea felt out of left field. For Carmella, it was a necessary step toward healing. Plus, hadn't Elsa said that their entire nuclear family had needed to heal but just hadn't been fully equipped enough to do it?

"Okay. We can try it," Elsa replied, giving her sister an assured smile.

"That's all anything is, right? Just trying to move forward. Failing and trying again."

Elsa squeezed her eyes tightly closed. "I hear Janine and Nancy say those types of things to our clients all the time. It difficult for me to take the advice to heart. Sometimes, it just feels like something we sell to the masses rather than something I fully believe in. I guess we should implement what we teach."

"It's real, Elsa. It has to be," Carmella breathed. "It's what the Lodge stands for. It's — it's what Dad worked for all these years."

"But he hurt you, so, so badly."

Carmella nodded. "People hurt people. It's a fact of life."

There was the vibrant cry of Zachery from down the hallway. Elsa and Carmella locked eyes in understanding that Lucas had arrived, which meant it was nearly time to attend the end of summer festival, located in downtown Edgartown.

"Can you believe it's already the end of summer festival?" Elsa asked as they walked side-by-side toward the foyer.

"In a way, it's been the longest summer of my life," Carmella said with a laugh.

"I know what you mean," Elsa said. "But I still want time to stop for just the slightest bit. Everything is in flux right now. Baby Zachery is only one and absolutely perfect. Mallory lives with me for the first time in years! And things with Bruce, well...."

Carmella jabbed Elsa in the side with her elbow. "Go on..."

"I don't know! Who ever knows what will happen next? All I can say is, this beginning part, with all the butterflies, dates, and text messaging, is exciting. I kind of forgot about the courting process. It was a million years ago with Aiden. That time was covered up with babies, diapers, mortgages and bills and all that. Now, I remember the magic of romance. It's totally blowing me away."

"I think I want to hear about this a whole lot more," Carmella said.

When they reached the foyer, they found the happy threesome, Mallory, Lucas and Zachery. Mallory had dressed Zachery up in a little sailing costume with blue and white stripes, and he buzzed his lips post-cry as though he had never exhibited such pain to the world. Lucas smiled at both Elsa and Carmella, with a lingering smile toward Elsa. Carmella sensed that he was still attempting to get into her good graces.

"Shall we head up to the festival?" Elsa asked. "Bruce plans to meet us there."

Janine whipped down the hall a moment later and cried, "I'm ready!" She then appeared in a beautiful light yellow frock with puffy sleeves and a cinched waist. She beamed at them and whipped her hair behind her shoulders. "Henry's meeting us there, too. I wish the girls could make it. Apparently, there's some huge event in Manhattan, of all places."

"Of all places," Elsa teased. "To hear you talk about New York, these days, it's like you've never even been there."

"Maybe it's true. You can take the girl out of the New York, and you can, actually, take the New York out of the girl?" Janine said.

"I don't know, either. That accent still comes through now and again," Carmella teased.

Janine cackled. "You got me there." Her smile was electric. Carmella reasoned that this was because Carmella wasn't frequently the one who cracked jokes or who teased others. This was because she had never felt such a level of comfort with anyone before.

Well, anyone but Cody, of course.

"How's the article doing?" Janine asked as they headed out the door.

"Oh, gosh, phenomenal," Elsa told her. "Did you read what Helen said?"

"I did," Janine replied. "She talked about the Lodge like it was heaven on earth."

"Yep. The phone's been ringing off the hook ever since it came out," Mallory affirmed. "We've filled up all the spots that had been canceled in the wake of Cal's article and we've booked ourselves solid till January if you can believe it."

"That's wonderful!" Elsa's cheeks hurt from smiling so much. She then flashed her eyes toward Carmella and said, "Sis, I can't thank you enough for saving the day. Seriously. That article was such a fantastic idea."

Carmella blushed. "I just hope that Cal read it. I hope he knew it was a direct attack from yours truly."

"Yes!" Janine hollered as she lifted her fist through the air and pumped it. "What a halfwit."

"He should know better than to mess with the Remington girls," Elsa smirked, then winked at her sister.

Carmella returned the smile, even as her stomach clenched strangely. It was a difficult thing for her, still reckoning the fact that she'd fallen for someone truly evil. Could she trust her instincts at all, moving forward? And what did it mean for her, now that Cody had abandoned her as a friend? Was she just poison?

The end of summer festival was in full swing. As usual, finding a parking spot was akin to finding a needle in a haystack. Everyone in the van — Janine, Carmella, Mallory, and Lucas yelped to the driver, Elsa, when they noted any sign of attack, any potential spot.

168

Finally, after twenty-five minutes of circling, they pulled into the abandoned spot of what seemed to be Jennifer Conrad's car, although Carmella couldn't be sure.

"Where's she off to?" Elsa asked, confirming it as she waved a hand toward Jennifer. "The party's only just begun!"

"We have to plan out our eating schedule for the night," Janine said as she stepped out of the van. "I've heard there's killer clam chowder at one of the kiosks. But I'm hankering for a corndog."

"A corndog!" Elsa cackled. "I haven't had a corndog in maybe twenty years?"

"Me neither. That's why I want it so bad," Janine affirmed. "I want to feel what it felt like to be twenty again without a care in the world. Heck, maybe I'll have two corndogs. Oh, look! There's Henry!"

Henry appeared on the right-hand side of what looked to be a cotton candy stand. He waved a hand and adjusted his hat as his eyes latched to Janine's. For a moment, it really was as if the two of them were just young lovers at the very beginning of their life and making plans to take on the world, side-by-side. Janine rushed up to him and wrapped her arms around his neck, then turned back to make sure the others followed along.

"She's so smitten, isn't she?" Elsa murmured under her breath.

"You think he's good enough for our Janine?" Carmella asked.

Elsa gave Carmella a surprised smile. "You know, I have begun to think of her that way. Bit-by-bit, she's become our Janine. Our other sister from another mother."

"It's weird, isn't it?" Carmella asked. "To have another sibling. For so long, it was just the two of us."

"Yes, it was just the two of us. And we hardly knew what to do with that."

They wandered through the many kiosks that were set up with various different foods and drink — the pulled pork sandwiches and shrimp tacos and clam chowder and locally-brewed beer and wine. Laughter seemed endless as it curled out from every nook and cranny and created a cacophony of song around them. Carmella selected a glass of wine from a local vendor and then laced her arm through Elsa's, just as Elsa pointed forward toward Bruce, there off to the side of a crowd that had gathered near the concert stage.

"There he is. That handsome man," Elsa breathed.

"Go get him, tiger," Carmella encouraged.

"Come with me," Elsa said. "I want you and Bruce to be friends too, you know."

"Of course. Sure. Yeah, let's go." Carmella felt slightly hesitant, even as she extended her stride alongside Elsa's. They breezed through the crowd, halting just once, as a little girl ducked out in front of them. Elsa pulled her foot back and let out a feigned screech.

"Ah! What is this creature in my path?"

The little girl erupted into giggles as though she'd done all of this on purpose. Carmella recognized the little girl immediately and knew in an instant that the girl had, in fact, done all this on purpose. For this little girl, this tiny mischievous thing before them was Gretchen, Cody's daughter.

"Gretchen! You little monkey," Carmella squealed, careful not to miss a beat. She dropped to a squat and caught Gretchen's eyes. "Where are you off to? Are you going to force your daddy to buy you all the cotton candy in the world?"

"Yes," Gretchen said, in that way she always did, where she stuck her tongue out the slightest bit and made a hissing sound.

Above her, Cody appeared, gasping for breath. "She's in a running phase," he explained. He, too, dropped to a squat, placed his hands tenderly around his daughter's stomach to support her, and remained careful not to make eye contact with Carmella.

"She's fast," Elsa said, impressed.

"She sure is. Already practicing for the track team," Cody replied.

Fiona appeared behind them after that. Carmella's heart cracked in two as the woman's eyes met hers. She stood from her squat and presented what Elsa would describe later as "the fakest smile" she'd ever seen.

"Hi, Fiona. It's been a long time."

Fiona stepped forward with two beers in hand. "Carmella. Elsa. Good to see you two again. Code, I got you an IPA."

"Thanks." Cody took the bottle and lifted it as his right hand dropped down to latch around Gretchen's.

"Are you guys having a good time?" Fiona asked. Her eyes remained directed toward Elsa, as though looking at Carmella was akin to looking at the sun.

"We are. Haven't been here long," Elsa said. Elsa was the queen of small talk — something Carmella had never mastered nor understood. Cody knew this about her. He seemed not to care so much right then.

But even now, he still refused to make eye contact with her. He continued to look back toward Fiona. Had they rekindled their romance? Had they decided to try again?

Carmella considered turning out from the crowd and marching

directly into the sea just for the slightest moment, but then came back to reality.

Gretchen tugged at her father's hand with excitement. Fiona laughed in that beautiful way of hers, a way Carmella had always been jealous of, and said, "You know what it's like with a toddler. We have to go where she wants to go. At least until we can convince her to go to sleep for the night."

We! They would be there, together, to put her to sleep for the night! Carmella felt shattered. She forced another smile and said, "Enjoy the festival." They then swept around Elsa and Carmella as her knees clacked together and her legs threatened to take her to the pavement below.

Elsa waited a moment before she drudged up the words.

"What the heck was that?"

Carmella shook her head. "I don't know."

"Did you and Cody have a falling out?"

"I don't really know."

"Um. What?"

Carmella heaved a sigh. Bruce appeared before them and dotted a kiss on Elsa's cheek in greeting. All the while, Elsa's eyes remained on Carmella's.

"He'll get over it. Whatever it is," Elsa said.

"Who will get over what?" Bruce asked.

Elsa's hand spread across Bruce's chest. Her lip puckered out with sorrow. "I'm just so sorry, Carmella."

"Don't worry about it," Carmella sounded defeated. "Really. Let's just enjoy the festival."

But Elsa's face remained stern. It was the face of an older sister who'd just learned someone was hurting her baby sister. Regardless of what had happened between them, that face would always make a reappearance. It was just the way things were, as expected as the blue sky above.

CHAPTER TWENTY-TWO

JUST BEFORE CARMELLA and Elsa planned to leave the Lodge to head to their first joint therapy session, there was a knock at the door of Carmella's office. Carmella assumed it was Elsa and called, "Come in! I'll be done in a second!" as she busied herself with a to-do list at her desk.

But the woman who appeared in the crack of the doorway wore a dark hood, thick sunglasses, and thigh-high boots. Her hair was tucked behind the hood, and the sunglasses were so enormous that it took Carmella a long moment to fully comprehend who had come to see her.

"Helen!"

Helen ducked into the office and clipped the door closed. "My bodyguard wants to kill me for making him come back over here. He had the car waiting and everything. But I felt I couldn't leave this place without saying goodbye to you."

Carmella's heart swelled. She rushed toward this woman — this acclaimed actress with more money than God, and flung her arms around her as though they were just kids on a playground. Helen's laugh was one of surprise. She patted Carmella's shoulder gently, then stepped the slightest bit back as she tilted her sunglasses toward the tip of her nose.

"It was so wonderful to live in the silence of myself down there by the waters of the Katama Bay for a while," she admitted. "Your sisters and stepmother were a tremendous help. But now that I think about it— when I looked in your eyes that day we went sailing, I finally understood the sadness within myself that I hadn't been able to fully see before. And maybe that's all life is. Figuring out our problems and having the courage to face them head-on. I don't know."

"I'm so happy for you, Helen. What's next for you?" Carmella asked.

"I'll fly to Los Angeles this evening," Helen said. "I have a house there. Wes Anderson wants to meet next week to discuss his next project. Quirky stuff, you know. Maybe that would suit me right now, something more soft and beautiful. I can't imagine sinking my teeth into something dramatic and emotional right now. All the pain from the miscarriage and the divorce will have to wait to be fit into my artistic side of things. Maybe I have to live in it for a bit longer."

Carmella gripped Helen's hand. It was difficult for her to imagine the next time she would see her. She bet it would on the cinema screen, blown up to ten times her real height. How strange that their paths had crossed in this way.

"I don't know if I can ever thank you enough for what you did with the article," Carmella finally said. She knew her words didn't express enough of the gratitude she felt.

"It was the truth," Helen returned softly. "What you and your family are doing here is remarkable and really needed. I plan on coming back sooner than later."

Carmella gave her a sneaky smile. "I can't wait. You're one special lady, Helen."

"Thank you. You as well, Carmella," Helen affirmed. "Just know that saying something to support you was the easiest thing in the world for me. I'm glad I did it."

Carmella watched Helen drop into the back of the limousine. It seemed that the paparazzi had cleared out already; there wasn't any sign of them peeping out from behind the line of trees in the woods. Carmella wondered about Cal, where he'd ended up, and if he now terrorized some other family or star. "Don't give in to that handsome smile," she breathed to no one in particular — to the wind, to the sky, to the trees.

"You ready?" Elsa appeared behind her, latching up her cardigan's buttons.

"Ready as I'll ever be," Carmella affirmed. "Just let me grab my purse."

As was tradition, Elsa drove them. Carmella could hardly remember a single time in their lives when Carmella had been in the driver's seat. Carmella dropped her head back and remained silent. Her thoughts toyed over what she might say at therapy and how she had to keep everything at a certain tone, a certain level, to ensure that Elsa's feelings weren't hurt.

As though Elsa could read Carmella's mind, she gripped the

steering wheel hard and whispered, "I just have no idea what to say at things like this."

"She normally just says to speak from the heart."

"But what if I don't have one?" Elsa laughed.

"That's about the most ridiculous thing I've ever heard," Carmella returned. "You have three times the heart of anyone else I know."

Carmella's therapist, Hannah, awaited them in the foyer of the office and then led them into the small, shadowed room. There were two cushioned chairs in front of a wooden one, where Hannah perched now. She splayed her hand out and beckoned for the sisters to sit.

Elsa adjusted her purse on her lap and then seemed to think better of it and place it at the side, on the floor. Carmella crossed and uncrossed her leg as her nervousness shined through.

"Elsa, it's good to finally meet you," Hannah said. "Carmella has told me a great deal about you. But I would love to know more about you in your own words."

All the color drained from Elsa's cheeks. She flashed her eyes toward Carmella with confusion and then breathed, "I don't know where to start."

"Anywhere you'd like. There are no wrong answers here."

Elsa cleared her throat. "Well, I guess, in a way, we're here because of my little brother, Colton." Her voice broke as she said his name.

Hannah nodded but didn't speak.

"It was a horrible accident. I was a teenager. My two siblings, brother and sister, were younger than me and were best friends. Sometimes, I was jealous of their relationship. They were just so close. It was like they had their own secret relationship. But slowly, around that time, I noticed that Carmella was trying to copy me a lot."

Carmella could hardly believe her ears. Was Elsa really just laying it all out for the therapist to hear? These weren't things Elsa had said to Carmella, ever. Here it was: finally, the truth. Could Carmella handle it?

"She wanted to be a teenager, like me and she wanted to wear makeup and try on my clothes and yada yada yada. It was sweet in a way, but I just wanted my own space."

"That makes so much sense," Hannah said. "Carmella, do you remember that?"

"Of course," Carmella affirmed. 'I thought you were the coolest girl in the entire world."

Elsa's eyes glowed with tears. "When Colton died, and I saw how much you blamed yourself and how Mom and Dad went so dark — I didn't know what to do. And maybe, maybe I wasn't so nice to you all the time, either. But I had my own issues that I was dealing with."

Carmella nodded. "I know. It wasn't easy on any of us."

"You heard me telling Bruce about the nights when I found you. When you were still asleep but crying about Colton," Elsa said.

Carmella nodded.

"All I wanted to do was tell you that everything would be okay, but back then, I didn't really believe it. I only started to believe it when I met Aiden and had my babies. But it didn't fully occur to me until recently that you were never allowed that reprieve. Gosh, Carmella, I just hope you know that I always wanted so much for you! I wanted the world for you! And I still do—"

Elsa reached out and gripped Carmella's hand so hard that her bones crackled. Carmella let out a sob.

"Carmella. How does it feel to hear your sister say all of that?"

"Ridiculous," Carmella finally said. "It feels ridiculous. Because I just never imagined that we would ever get to a point where we could say actual truths to one another. It's the greatest thing in the world — and it feels like a fantasy."

The conversation continued. Eventually, they shifted gears toward their mother and father, and then Karen, the demon herself.

"I just really thought you pushed her away from me because you didn't want me to be happy," Carmella confessed.

"Not at all. I saw what she was doing to us, to Dad, to our family, and I had to do something to stop it," Elsa said. She then brushed a tear from her cheek and said, "I can't believe you saw her in New Mexico. I would have fallen to the floor."

"I almost did."

"I Googled her recently," Elsa said. "Read about her clinic in Wisconsin. And also about a drunk driving ticket in Denver and a little money scheme in Connecticut. It seems Karen has made the rounds over the years."

"She really does take and take and take," Carmella whispered. "I can't believe I fell for it."

"Again, ladies, you two were just teenagers at the time," Hannah interjected. "You can't be too hard on yourself. You were taking the information you had at the time and doing your best with it."

"We were doing our best," Carmella breathed.

"And I guess, in a way, we still are," Elsa affirmed. "As difficult as that is to grasp sometimes."

After the first therapy session was over, Hannah arranged for them to return the week after that. "We'll keep this going a few more months at least," she suggested and the girls agreed. "That's what I would recommend. And Elsa, if you're at all interested in personal therapy, please let me know. You can either work with one of my colleagues or me."

Back in Elsa's car, Elsa heaved a sigh and said, "Therapy. I never thought I'd see the day."

"What did you think?"

"It's not so bad. I think it will really help, although it's difficult to say so soon out of the gate."

"Yeah. I didn't feel any real weight off my shoulders for a while. But it slowly feels like peeling layers from an onion or something. Eventually, I started to feel like myself again for the first time."

Elsa sniffled, gripped a Kleenex, and then mopped herself up. "I think this calls for a glass of wine. Maybe at The Hesson House? They have such a beautiful view."

"That's a deal."

Elsa drove them north of Edgartown, to the old mansion, with its long driveway lined with huge old oak trees. They parked in the drive and then walked around the westward side of the house, where a maître d' welcomed them and then led them to a little table by the water. To Carmella and Elsa's delight, Lola was seated along the sand with her daughter, Audrey. Audrey was in the midst of telling what seemed to be a raucous story — one so wild that a bit of lipstick had wound up on her chin.

"Hello, ladies!" Carmella greeted with a smile.

Lola grinned broadly, reached for a napkin, and smeared it across Audrey's chin.

"Audrey just came back for a visit. She's been back at Penn State for a week. And she has so many crazy stories," Lola said.

Audrey gestured under the table, where her baby, Max Sheridan, was deep in sleep. "I just couldn't bear to be away for much longer."

Carmella and Elsa sat at a nearby table and ordered a bottle of Pinot Grigio. They clinked glasses and studied one another in silence.

"What will it be like to be back to our healthy selves?" Elsa asked suddenly as a smile lifted across her cheeks.

"It should be a wild ride," Carmella affirmed. "I guess we'll know it when we get there."

Elsa sniffled, then positioned herself far back in her chair. "Do you remember that song Colton used to sing all the time?"

Carmella clamped her eyes shut as memories flew through her mind. "*Don't Stop Me Now by Queen.* Right?"

"He was obsessed," Elsa stated. "He ran around the living room, up and down the beach, singing at the top of his lungs. I thought he was the most annoying little boy the world had ever created. But now, whenever I hear that song, I can't help but dance around, just like him, and smile to myself."

"I had no idea you remembered that," Carmella breathed.

Elsa nodded. "I remember all of it. And I loved every single minute. I plan to love the rest of it, too. If you're game to create more memories with me."

CHAPTER TWENTY-THREE

YOU HAD to take risks in life. Carmella had read this fact over and over again — yet never fully taken it to heart. Here, in her tiny apartment, as she arranged the silliest decoration across a chocolate cake, she wondered if this was the kind of "risk" they'd meant when they had said this now-famous phrase.

"I'M SORRY." The words were scribed across the cake in Scrabble letters, another game she and Cody had frequently played throughout their teenage years, as they hadn't had anyone else to hang with or anywhere else to go. The cake was homemade, specifically by Carmella herself. She had considered hiring out to the likes of Christine Sheridan or Jennifer Conrad, but she wanted this particular sweet treat to come straight from the heart. If it was lackluster, so be it. They could laugh about it while they tossed it in the trash and went for milkshakes.

At least, she hoped for that sort of laughter again. She ached for the sound of Cody's laugh. It had been so long since she'd heard it.

Was it creepy to wait outside of his work for him to leave? Carmella wasn't sure. It was certainly up there on the creepiness scale — maybe right behind stalking, although was it really stalking if you already knew the person so well that you understood their schedule to a T? She wasn't sure about that, either. She hoped, when she outlined what she'd done later for her therapist, Hannah wouldn't make a face and say, "Yes. Creepy. Don't do that again," and then jot another note on her notepad. But there was a chance, she supposed.

A benefit, too, of the cake was that she could eat it alone in the sadness of her house if Cody told her he really never wanted to see her again. If that happened, then she could find solace in sugar and sleep.

Carmella felt like an exposed nerve, there beneath the oak tree outside of Cody's work. She held the cake aloft and nodded at random to the various colleagues Cody had introduced her to over the years. In fact, more than one of them had attempted to date her. She remembered it — Cody telling her, his eyes darkening, that he could match her with one of his co-workers if she wanted that. She had always declined. And maybe, just maybe, he'd always breathed a sigh of relief.

Gosh, she missed him. She missed him more than stars in the sky and droplets of water in the ocean.

"Carmella?"

Somehow, in all her wild daydreams, she had missed the fact that he'd exited the building. He now stood before her — all six-foot-three of him, broad shoulders, his thick hair disheveled and his eyes sparkling with kindness, even as his face was marred with confusion. She instinctively lifted the cake, feeling foolish at that moment, because she wanted to show him the Scrabble letters that read: "I'M SORRY." And after all, she was really sorry. But just then, she couldn't form the words.

"Huh." He eyed the cake and then found her gaze. "I wish I could say it was beautiful." There it was: that sneaky smile.

"No. But it has a lot of heart."

"You're saying that cakes are worth more than their beauty? That it's more about what's inside that counts?" he teased.

"Something like that."

Carmella hadn't envisioned this next part. In fact, in most scenarios in her head, she'd imagined Cody looking her way and then storming off. Yes, in most versions of her cake scenario, she was halfway through her second slice and preparing herself for a sugar overload.

"Maybe we could talk. And I can put this in my car."

"Okay."

Cody walked Carmella back to her car. He stood off to the side while she placed the cake on the passenger side. When she drew the door closed, her eyes met his, and then he dropped her gaze. Awkward was too weak of a word for what this was.

"Maybe we could walk by the water?" Carmella suggested.

Cody led them in that direction. Carmella found herself studying his profile — the elegant swoop of his nose, his luscious lips. Had she never noticed how handsome he was before, or had she just shoved these thoughts from her mind? It was a funny thing, the human mind. It could build up boundaries even without you knowing about them. How much control did anyone truly have over what they did, over who they loved?

Cody paused at the fence and leaned against it. He stared down at the water as it rushed against the side of the rocks and frothed up. As kids, they'd made up little stories about the froth as though the ocean was a kind of dessert.

"We're not back together, by the way," Cody said finally. "Me and Fiona."

Carmella's throat nearly closed up.

"I figured you'd think we were after you saw us at the festival. But she asked if I would help out with Gretchen that night, and I said, of course, yes. To be honest, it was kind of cool. To be there, just the three of us, but when I saw you — I knew I didn't handle it well. I'm sorry."

Carmella shook her head that her hair swished across her ears. She wasn't fully sure what to say. She placed her hand over her lips and told herself not to cry. Tears came anyway.

"I want you to be with her if you want to be with her," Carmella breathed as her voice broke off to a whisper. "I really mean that."

"Well, I don't want that."

Carmella blinked up at him. "Are you sure?"

"Yes, I am."

Carmella returned her gaze to the water. How could she say all the things she wanted to say? How could she translate decades of whatever this relationship had meant to her?

"You're right, you know," Carmella murmured.

"About what?"

"About my selfishness. I was so obsessed with my own heartache for so long that I really struggled to see anyone else's. No wonder you broke that day. I pushed you for years toward that breaking point," Carmella said.

Cody shook his head. "No. What I said was wrong."

"It wasn't. But there's more. Cody, for years, I haven't known how to love anyone because I haven't really known how to love myself. I don't know how long that journey toward self-love will take. My therapist can't give me a number, unfortunately."

Cody cracked the slightest of smiles.

"I want to try. I want to try to be myself, or at least a version of myself that we both can stand. And I was wondering if — if it was too late? If maybe I've missed every chance? If maybe you don't want to at least try?"

Cody's eyes were wet with tears. Suddenly, his arms were around her; his lips found hers. How strange and how beautiful it was. His scent, his warmth — it was all so familiar, but there was more to it, an excitement, a sizzling energy that she hadn't anticipated. His lips were so soft, so tender, and they seemed to ache with longing for her. He pressed his body tightly against hers. And when their kiss broke, he continued to hold his nose against hers as he whispered, "You know, I've wanted to do that for thirty years, or so. That was the longest wait in the world."

Carmella and Cody found themselves in the car an hour later. They had torn into the cake, which Cody had declared, "Absolutely passable." They licked chocolate crumbs from the fork tongs and kissed between bites. Carmella genuinely felt that she was lost in his eyes.

"So, one final question," Cody said as he dug his fork into the cake once more.

"What's that?"

"Will you go to prom with me?"

Carmella laughed toward the night sky. "I already did. You were my date, dummy."

"Yeah. But you wouldn't let me dance with you. Not properly."

Carmella stuck her tongue into the side of her cheek as memory of that night fell over her. "I wanted to."

"You did?"

"Yes, but it seemed so lame," Carmella confessed. "Now, I wish I had that memory."

"I'll dance with you soon. I know it."

"Maggie's wedding is coming up."

"Janine's daughter?"

"The very one."

"Won't that wedding be really ritzy with loads of Manhattan socialites?"

"I just pray to God that Janine's ex-best friend, who stole her husband, doesn't show up," Carmella stated.

"Sounds like a wild ride. I'm in!"

Carmella curled her head against his chest and exhaled somberly. What was it about falling in love that made her so in-tune with her emotions? She felt every ache, every sadness, and every happiness. She was ever-changing like a storm.

"I really do love you, Cody," she breathed.

"I love you, too, Carmella."

CHAPTER TWENTY-FOUR

"CODY. I think this time the task is yours." Bruce extended his arm and, with it, an enormous spatula that he had planned to use to flip the burgers. Apparently, Susan Sheridan, his boss, had some kind of emergency in Oak Bluffs, where he worked at the law office. He wagged his eyebrows and said, "It's up to you to feed the Remington girls. I don't know if you can handle it. But you have to give it your all."

Cody stepped forward and gripped the spatula. His eyes feigned sternness. "I'll do my very best, sir."

"Your best isn't good enough!" Bruce cried before he smacked him across the back and said, "I'm really sorry to leave, everyone! Save me a burger?"

"Of course," Elsa said. She stood and kissed him gently, then said, "Don't work too hard, okay? That Susan Sheridan really has the whip on you."

"She's a good egg, really," Bruce affirmed. "She's an extremely hard worker. One that crams more hours in the day than anyone I know."

Carmella stood alongside the grill and watched as Cody splayed a spatula across the browning meat, then sent one of the little disks toward the sky. He wagged his eyebrows and said, "What do you think? Think I'll be accepted into the family with these flipping skills?"

"Oh, come on, Cody. You were already going to be accepted into the family," Elsa said, feigning sarcasm.

Janine entered from the living room and hollered her own greeting, a glass of wine in hand. "I swear that wedding can just go ahead and happen already. I'm so done! One fire after another."

"Hopefully not literal fires?" Nancy asked. She sat alongside Janine and furrowed her brow.

"Not yet," Janine affirmed. She lowered her voice, then added, "Apparently, Alyssa told her father that he couldn't bring his new, you know, girlfriend. And he lost it and screamed and said that he is paying for the wedding, which is true. It just totally overwhelms me, thinking about all of this happening at home. I mean, at home in Manhattan. This is my home, now."

Nancy patted the top of her hand. "That's right. This is your home. All that chaos over there in the city has nothing to do with you, now. And besides—"

At that moment, Henry marched through the screen door. He held his video camera and directed it toward Janine as he put on a mocking, old-world television announcer voice. "And here, over here, we have the world-famous Janine Grimson, a woman of such remarkable grace and poise and artistry that she puts even the likes of Marilyn Monroe to shame."

Janine blushed like a teenager. Cody arched an eyebrow and caught Carmella's eye. She drew up to her tip-toes and kissed him on the lips, just as Elsa strode past and snapped her fingers. "Don't pay attention to Carmella, Cody. Pay attention to the burgers. We have a huge family to feed— all very hungry with huge stomachs to fill."

"No pressure, huh," Cody joked. "I understand." Just then, Cody's phone buzzed. He winced and said, "That's Fiona. She said she'd be dropping Gretchen off around now. But—" He nodded toward the spatula and the pinkish-brown burgers.

"I'll go get her," Carmella offered as brightly as she could. "I don't mind."

"Are you sure?"

"Of course."

Carmella bounded through the house and then headed out the front door. Sure enough, Fiona's car sat out front, the engine still humming. Fiona was halfway into the back seat, where she unbuckled Gretchen's car seat, then whipped her out into the beautiful late summer air. When she placed Gretchen's feet in the grass, her eyes found Carmella's. She flinched.

"Hi there." Fiona stepped forward, her hand still wrapped around Gretchen's hand.

"Hi." Carmella stepped closer. What the heck was she supposed to say? Did this woman hate her?

"Cody told me about you guys," Fiona said.

Carmella nodded.

"And I told him — finally."

Carmella's eyebrows rose. "Really?"

"Yes. It was always so clear to me about you two. It made me so jealous for a long time, but now, I think it's better this way. And Gretchen already adores you. That's the most important thing to me, you know? That I know who's with my child. Think of it. If Cody and I had gotten divorced, which was probably inevitable anyway and then he'd ended up with some random woman I hated? That would have been awful."

"Cody wouldn't have done that to you," Carmella said.

"You're right. He's not that kind of guy," Fiona agreed. After a pause, she added, "He's actually the best kind of guy. And I think I was too dumb to treat him right."

Carmella shook her head. "It took me thirty years to realize that we should even try."

"Well, I'm damn glad for that. We wouldn't have Gretchen if you'd jumped the gun," Fiona said. This time, she gave the slightest of smiles.

Carmella was so grateful for that.

Carmella gathered Gretchen up in her arms and said goodbye to Fiona, who got in her car and sped off toward her own house, which was probably empty. Carmella couldn't help but think of Fiona and her loneliness as she was allowed to enter back into the throng of loud voices, loads of various types of food — so much that they all stuffed themselves silly for the next few hours and then eventually went back for more.

Gretchen lifted a little tube of bubbles and blew long and hard as big, boisterous bubbles flew out from the little bubble wand. Each time, Nancy and Elsa and Carmella clapped for the bubbles, and they floated out toward the sand and the water beyond. After twenty minutes, Gretchen accidentally spilled the bubble liquid across the porch. Tears were shed, but soon, Carmella gathered

Gretchen on her lap and pointed out toward a bright light on the horizon line.

"Do you know what that is?"

Gretchen shook her head.

"It's a boat. It's sailing across the waters toward home. And do you want to know what they're doing on that boat right now?"

"Yes."

"They're blowing bubbles, just like you. And those bubbles are floating up and up, into the starry sky."

"Really?" Gretchen looked mesmerized.

"Yes. And they're competing to see which of them can blow the biggest bubbles."

"Wow." Gretchen's eyelids slowly dripped toward her cheeks.

Cody grinned and gestured toward the others, telling them with his eyes that Gretchen had fallen asleep. Slowly, Carmella rose, carrying Gretchen's little body toward the screen door. Just before she entered, she caught Elsa's eye.

"I remember when Mom used to carry you just like that from this very porch," Elsa said then, just soft enough for only Carmella to hear.

The words painted the most glorious picture.

For the first time ever, Carmella felt a part of a greater circle of events — of life, love, childhood memories and death. It was all connected. She wasn't alone anymore.

Upstairs, Cody and Carmella placed Gretchen at the center of the bed and then layout on either side of her, listening to the soft rise and fall of her breath.

"Can you believe we met each other not long after her age?" Carmella asked.

"We had no idea what we were getting into," Cody affirmed.

"Do you think we know what we're getting into, now?"

Cody shifted his head so that he peered at Carmella through the grey shadows that separated them. "No. But I like not knowing."

"It doesn't scare you?"

"Everything scares me."

"Me too."

"But I think everything scares everyone," Cody whispered.

Above Gretchen's head, Cody splayed his hand out across the pillow. Carmella linked her fingers with his. They held hands like that in the dark as Gretchen slept gently alongside them. It was the end of summer, yet the start of so many things. The only thing left to do now was soar.

OTHER BOOKS BY KATIE

———

The Vineyard Sunset Series

Sisters of Edgartown Series

Secrets of Mackinac Island Series

A Katama Bay Series